CIVILIZATION

Tales of the Orient

ELLEN N. LA MOTTE

Civilization

Ellen Newbold La Motte

© 1st World Library, 2007
PO Box 2211
Fairfield, IA 52556
www.1stworldlibrary.com
First Edition

LCCN: 2007920640

Softcover ISBN: 978-1-4218-3951-6
Hardcover ISBN: 978-1-4218-3851-9
eBook ISBN: 978-1-4218-4051-2

Purchase *"Civilization"*
as a traditional bound book at:
www.1stWorldLibrary.com/purchase.asp?ISBN=978-1-4218-3951-6

1st World Library is a literary, educational organization
dedicated to:

- Creating a free internet library of downloadable ebooks

- Hosting writing competitions and offering book
  publishing scholarships.

Interested in more 1st World Library books?
contact: literacy@1stworldlibrary.com
Check us out at: www.1stworldlibrary.com

1ˢᵗ World Library Literary Society

Giving Back to the World

"If you want to work on the core problem, it's early school literacy."

- James Barksdale, former CEO of Netscape

"No skill is more crucial to the future of a child, or to a democratic and prosperous society, than literacy."

- Los Angeles Times

Literacy... means far more than learning how to read and write... The aim is to transmit... knowledge and promote social participation."

- UNESCO

"Literacy is not a luxury, it is a right and a responsibility. If our world is to meet the challenges of the twenty-first century we must harness the energy and creativity of all our citizens."

- President Bill Clinton

"Parents should be encouraged to read to their children, and teachers should be equipped with all available techniques for teaching literacy, so the varying needs and capacities of individual kids can be taken into account."

- Hugh Mackay

CONTENTS

THE YELLOW STREAK

He came out to Shanghai a generation ago, in those days when Shanghai was not as respectable as it is now—whatever that says to you. It was, of course, a great change from Home, and its crude pleasures and crude companions gave him somewhat of a shock. For he was of decent stock, with a certain sense of the fitness of things, and the beach-combers, adventurers, rough traders and general riff-raff of the China Coast, gathered in Shanghai, did not offer him the society he desired. He was often obliged to associate with them, however, more or less, in a business way, for his humble position as minor clerk in a big corporation entailed certain responsibilities out of hours, and this responsibility he could not shirk, for fear of losing his position. Thus, by these acts of civility, more or less enforced, he was often led into a loose sort of intimacy, into companionship with people who were distasteful to his rather fastidious nature. But what can you expect on the China Coast? He was rather an upright sort of young man, delicate and abstemious, and the East being new to him, shocked him. He took pleasure in walking along the Bund, marvelling at the great river full of the ships of the world, marvelling at the crowds from the four corners of the world who disembarked from these ships and scattered along the broad and sunny thoroughfare, seeking amusements of a primitive sort. But in these amusements he took no part. For himself, a gentleman, they did not attract. Not for long. The sing-song girls and the "American girls" were coarse, vulgar creatures and he did not like them. It was no better in the back streets—bars and saloons, gaming houses and opium divans, all the coarse paraphernalia of pleasure, as the China Coast understood the word, left him unmoved. These things had little influence upon him, and the men who liked them overmuch, who chaffed him because of his squeamishness and distaste of them, were not such friends as he needed in his life. However, there were few alternatives. There was almost nothing else for it. Companionship of this kind, or the absolute loneliness of a hotel bedroom were the alternatives which confronted him. He had very little money,—just a modest salary—therefore the excitement of trading, of big, shady deals, said nothing to him. He went to the races, a shy onlooker. He could not afford to risk his little salary in betting. Above all things, he was cautious. Consequently life did not offer him much outside of office hours, and in office hours it offered him nothing at all. You will see from this that he was a very limited person, incapable of expansion. Now as a rule, life in the Far East does not have this effect upon young men. It is generally stimulating and exciting, even to the most unimaginative, while the novelty of it, the utter freedom and lack of restraint and absence of conventional public opinion is such that usually, within a very short time, one becomes unfitted to return to a more formal society. In the old days of a generation ago, life on the China Coast was probably much more exciting and inciting than it is to-day, although to-day, in all conscience, the checks are off. But our young man was rather fine, rather extraordinarily fastidious, and moreover, he had a very healthy young appetite for the normal. The offscourings of the world and of society rolled into Shanghai with the inflow of each yellow tide of the Yangtzse, and somehow, he resented that deposit. He resented it, because from that deposit he must pick out his friends. Therefore instead of accepting the situation, instead of drinking himself into acquiescence, or drugging himself into acquiescence, he found himself quite resolved to remain firmly and consciously outside of it. In consequence of which decision he remained homesick and lonely, and his presence in the community was soon forgotten or overlooked. Shy and priggish, he continued to lead his lonely life. In his solitary walks along the Bund, there was no one to take his arm and snigger suggestions into his ear, and lead him into an open doorway where the suggestions could be carried out. He had come out to the East for a long term of years, and the prospect of these interminable years made his position worse. Not that it shook his decision to remain aloof and detached from the call of the East—his decision was not shaken in the slightest, which seemed almost a pity.

Like all foreigners, of course, he had his own opinions of the Chinese. They were an inferior, yellow race, and therefore despicable. But having also a firm, unshakable opinion of his own race, especially of those individuals of his race in which a yellow streak predominated, he held the Chinese in no way inferior to these yellow-streaked individuals. Which argues broadmindedness and fairmindedness. Of the two, perhaps, he thought the Chinese preferable—under certain circumstances. Yet he knew them to be irritating in business dealings, corrupt, dishonest—on the whole he felt profound scorn for them. But as they had been made to suit the purposes of the ruling races of the world—such, for example, as himself, untainted by a yellow streak—he had to that extent, at least, succumbed to the current opinions of Shanghai. He resolved to make use of them—of one, at least, in particular.

He wanted a home. Wanted it desperately. He wanted to indulge his quiet, domestic tastes, to live in peace a normal, peaceful life, far apart from the glittering trivialities of the back streets of the town. He wanted a home of his own, a refuge to turn to at the end of each long, monotonous day. You see, he was not an adventurer, a gambler, a wastrel, and he wanted a quiet home with a companion to greet him, to take care of him, to serve him in many ways. There was no girl in England whom he wanted to come out to marry him. Had there been such a girl, he would probably not have allowed her to come. He was a decent young man, and the climate was such, here on the China Coast, that few women could stand it without more of the comforts and luxury than his small salary could have paid for. So finally, at the end of a year or two, he got himself the home he wanted, in partnership with a little Chinese girl who answered every purpose. He was not in love with her, in any exalted sense, but she supplied certain needs, and at the end of his long days, he had the refuge that he craved. She kept him from going to the bad.

His few friends—friends, however, being hardly the word to apply to his few casual acquaintances,—were greatly surprised at this. Such an establishment seemed to them the last sort of thing a man of this type would have gone in for. He had seemed such a decent sort, too. Really, a few professed to be quite shocked—they said you never knew how the East would affect a person, especially a decent person. For themselves, they preferred looser bonds, with less responsibility. They said this to each other between drinks, and there was then, as now, much drinking in Shanghai. A few even said this to each other quite seriously, as they lay in pairs on opium divans, smoking opium, with little Chinese girls filling their pipes—girls who would afterwards be as complaisant as was required. One man who had lost his last cent at the gambling wheels, professed great astonishment at this departure from the usual track, a departure quite unnecessary since there were so many ways of amusing oneself out here in the East. Of course such unions were common enough, heaven knows—there was nothing unusual about it. But then such fastidious people did not as a rule go in for them. It was not the menage, it was the fact that this particular young man had set up such, that caused the comment. The comment, however, was short-lived. There was too much else to think about.

Rogers liked his new life very much. Never for a moment did he think of marrying the girl. That, of course, never dawned on him. Recollect, he was in all things decent and correct, and such a step would have been suicidal. Until the time came for him to go Home, she was merely being made use of—and to be useful to the ruling races is the main object in life for the Chinese. They exist for the profit and benefit of the superior races, and this is the correct, standard opinion of their value, and there are few on the China Coast, from Hongkong upwards, who will disagree with it.

In time, a son was born to Rogers, and for a while it filled him with dismay. It was a contingency he had not foreseen, a responsibility he had not contemplated, had not even thought he could afford. But in time he grew used to the boy, and, in a vague way, fond of him. He disturbed him very little, and counted very little in his life, after all. Later, as the years rolled by, he began to feel some responsibility towards the child. He despised half-breeds, naturally—every one does. They are worse than natives, having inherited the weakness of both ancestries. He was sincerely glad to be rid of the whole business, when, at the end of about fifteen years, he was called home to England. It had all served his purpose, this establishment of his, and thanks to it, he was still clean and straight, undemoralised by the insidious, undermining influences of the East. When he returned to his native land, he could find himself a home upon orthodox lines and live happily ever afterwards. Before he left Shanghai, he sent his little Chinese girl, a woman long ago, of course, back to her native province in the interior, well supplied with money and with the household furniture. For the boy he had arranged everything. He was to be educated in some good, commercial way, fitted to take care of himself in the future. Through his lawyer, he set aside a certain sum for this purpose, to be expended annually until the lad was old enough to earn his own living. In all ways Rogers was thoughtful and decent, far-sighted and provident. No one could accuse him of selfishness. He did not desert his woman, turn her adrift unprovided for, as many another would have done. No, thank heavens, he thought to himself as he leaned over the rail of the ship, fast making its way down the yellow tide, he had still preserved his sense of honour. So many men go to pieces out in the East, but he, somehow, had managed to keep himself clear and clean.

Rogers drops out of the tale at this point, and as the ship slips out of sight down the lower reaches of the Yangtzse, so does he disappear from this story. It is to the boy that we must now turn our attention, the half-caste boy who had received such a heritage of decency and honour from one side of his house. In passing, let it be also said that his mother, too, was a very decent little woman, in a humble, Chinese way, and that his inheritance from this despised Chinese side was not discreditable. His mother had gone obediently back to the provinces, as had been arranged, the house passed into other hands, and the half-caste boy was sent off to school somewhere, to finish his education. Being young, he consoled himself after a time for the loss of his home, its sudden and complete collapse. The memory of that home, however, left deep traces upon him.

In the first place, he was inordinately proud of his white blood. He did not know that it had cost his guardian considerable searching to find a school where white blood was not objected to—when running in Chinese veins. His schoolmates, of European blood, were less tolerant than the school authorities. He therefore soon found his white blood to be a curse. There is no need to go into this in detail. For every one who knows the East, knows the contempt that is shown a half-breed, a Eurasian. Neither fish, flesh nor fowl—an object of general distrust and disgust. Oh, useful enough in business circles, since they can usually speak both languages, which is, of course, an advantage. But socially, impossible. In time, he passed into a banking house, where certain of his qualities were appreciated, but outside of banking hours he was confronted with a worse problem than that which had beset his father. He felt himself too good for the Chinese. His mother's people did not appeal to him, he did not like their manners and customs. Above all things he wanted to be English, like his father, whom in his imagination he had magnified into a sort of god. But his father's people would have none of him. Even the clerks in the bank only spoke to him on necessary business, during business hours, and cut him dead on the street. As for the roysterers and beach-combers gathered in the bars of the hotels, they made him feel, low as they were, that they were not yet sunk low enough to enjoy such companionship as his. It was very depressing and made him feel very sad. He did not at first feel any resentment or bitterness towards his absent father, disappeared forever from his horizon. But it gave him a profound sense of depression. True, there were many other

Ellen Newbold La Motte

half-breeds for him to associate with—the China Coast is full of such—but they, like himself, were ambitious for the society of the white man. What he craved was the society of the white man, to which, from one side of his house, he was so justly entitled. He was not a very noticeable half-breed either, for his features were regular, and he was not darker than is compatible with a good sunburn. But just the same, it was unmistakable, this touch of the tar brush, to the discriminating European eye. He seemed inordinately slow witted—it took him a long time to realise his situation. He argued it out with himself constantly, and could arrive at no logical explanation. If his mother, pure Chinese, was good enough for his father, why was not he, only half-Chinese, good enough for his father's people? Especially in view of the fact that his father's history was by no means uncommon. His father and his kind had left behind them a trail of half-breeds—thousands of them. If his mother had been good enough for his father—His thoughts went round and round in a puzzled, enquiring circle, and still the problem remained unsolved. For he was very young, and not as yet experienced.

He was well educated. Why had his father seen to that? And he was well provided for, and was now making money on his own account. He bought very good clothes with his money, and went in the bar of one of the big hotels, beautifully dressed, and took a drink at the bar and looked round to see who would drink with him. He could never catch a responsive eye, so was forced to drink alone. He hated drinking, anyway. In many ways he was like his father. The petty clerks who were at the office failed to see him at the race course. He hated the races, anyway. In many respects he was like his father. But he was far more lonely than his father had ever been. Thus he went about very lonely, too proud to associate with the straight Chinese, his mother's people, and humbled and snubbed by the people of his father's race.

He was twenty years old when the Great War upset Europe. Shanghai was a mass of excitement. The newspapers were ablaze. Men were needed for the army. One of the clerks in the office resigned his post and went home to enlist. In the first rush of enthusiasm, many other young Englishmen in many other offices resigned their positions and enlisted, although not a large number of them did so. For it was inconceivable that the war could last more than a few weeks—when the first P. and O. boat reached London, it would doubtless all be over. During the excitement of those early days, some of the office force so far forgot themselves as to speak to him on the subject. They asked his opinion, what he thought of it. They did not ask the shroff, the Chinese accountant, what he thought of it. But they asked him. His heart warmed! They were speaking to him at last as an equal, as one who could understand, who knew things English, by reason of his English blood.

So the Autumn came, and still the papers continued full of appeals for men. No more of the office force enlisted, and their manner towards him, of cold indifference, was resumed again after the one outburst of friendliness occasioned by the first excitement. Still the papers contained their appeals for men. But the men in the other offices round town did not seem to enlist either. He marvelled a little. Doubtless, however, England was so great and so invincible that she did not need them. But why then these appeals? Soon he learned that these young men could not be spared from their offices in the Far East. They were indispensable to the trade of the mighty Empire. Still, he remained puzzled. One day, in a fit of boldness, he ventured to ask the young man at the next stool why he did not go. According to the papers, England was clamouring loudly for her sons.

"Enlist!" exclaimed the young Englishman angrily, colouring red. "Why don't you enlist yourself? You say you're an Englishman, I believe!"

The half-breed did not see the sneer. A great flood of light filled his soul. He was English! One half of him was English! England was calling for her own—and he was one of her own! He would answer the call. A high, hot wave of exultation passed over him. His spirit was uplifted, exalted. The glorious

Ellen Newbold La Motte

opportunity had come to prove himself—to answer the call of the blood! Why had he never thought of it before!

For days afterwards he went about in a dream of excitement, his soul dwelling on lofty heights. He asked to be released from his position, and his request was granted. The manager shook hands with him and wished him luck. His brother clerks nodded to him, on the day of his departure, and wished him a good voyage. They did not shake hands with him, and were not enthusiastic, as he hoped they would be. His spirits were a little dashed by their indifference. However, they had always slighted him, so it was nothing unusual. It would be different after he had proved himself—it would be all right after he had proved himself, had proved to himself and to them, that English blood ran in his veins, and that he was answering the call of the blood.

His adventures in the war do not concern us. They concern us no more than the gap in the office, caused by his departure, concerned his employer or his brother clerks. Within a few weeks, his place was taken by another young Englishman, just out, and the office routine went on as usual, and no one gave a thought to the young recruit who had gone to the war. Just one comment was made. "Rather cheeky of him, you know, fancying himself an Englishman." Then the matter dropped. Gambling and polo and golf and cocktails claimed the attention of those who remained, and life in Shanghai continued normal as usual.

In due course of time, his proving completed, he returned to his native land. As the ship dropped anchor in the lower harbour, his heart beat fast with a curious emotion. An unexpected emotion, Chinese in its reactions. The sight of the yellow, muddy Yangtzse moved him strangely. It was his river. It belonged, somehow, to him. He stood, a lonely figure, on the deck, clad in ill-fitting, civilian clothes, not nearly so jaunty as those he used to wear before he went away. His clothes fell away from him strangely, for illness had wasted him, and his collar stood out stiffly from his scrawny neck. One leg was gone, shot away above the knee, and he hobbled painfully down the gangplank and on to the tender, using his crutches very awkwardly.

The great, brown, muddy Yangtzse! His own river! The ships of the world lay anchored in the harbour, the ships of all the world! The tender made its way upward against the rushing tide, and great, clumsy junks floated downstream. As they neared the dock, crowds of bobbing sampans, with square, painted eyes—so that they might see where they were going—came out and surrounded them. A miserable emotion overcame him. They were his junks—he understood them. They were his sampans, with their square, painted eyes—eyes that the foreigners pointed to and laughed at! He understood them all—they were all his!

Presently he found himself upon the crowded Bund, surrounded by a crowd of men and women, laughing, joyous foreigners, who had come to meet their own from overseas. No one was there to meet him, but it was not surprising. He had sent word to no one, because he had no one to send word to. He was undecided where to go, and he hobbled along a little, to get out of the crowd, and to plan a little what he should do. As he stood there undecided, waiting a little, hanging upon his crutches, two young men came along, sleek, well-fed, laughing. He recognised them at once—two of his old colleagues in the office. They glanced in his direction, looked down on his pinned-up trouser leg, caught his eye, and then, without sign of recognition, passed on.

He was still a half-breed.

ON THE HEIGHTS

Rivers made his way to China many years ago. He was an adventurer, a ne'er-do-weel, and China in those days was just about good enough for him. Since he was English, it might have seemed more natural for him to have gone to India, or the Straits Settlements, or one of the other colonies of the mighty Empire, but for some reason, China drew him. He was more likely to meet his own sort in China, where no questions would be asked. And he did meet his own sort—people just like himself, other adventurers and ne'er-do-weels, and their companionship was no great benefit to him. So he drifted about all over China, around the coast towns and back into the interior, to and fro, searching for opportunities to make his fortune. But being the kind of man he was, fortune seemed always to elude him. In course of time he became rather well known on the China Coast—known as a beach-comber. And even when he went into the remote, interior province of Szechuan, where he lived a precarious, hand-to-mouth existence for several years, he was also known as a beach-comber. Which shows that being two thousand miles inland does not alter the characteristics associated with that name.

Personally, he was not a bad sort. Men liked him, that is, men of his own type. Some of them succeeded better than he did, and afterwards referred to him as "poor old Rivers," although he was not really old at that time. Neither was he really old either, when he died, several years later. He was rather interesting too, in a way, since he had experienced many adventures in the course of his wanderings in remote parts of the country, which adventures were rather tellable. He even knew a lot about China, too, which is more than most people do who have lived in China many years. Had he been of that sort, he might have written rather valuable books, containing his shrewd observations and intimate, underhand knowledge of political and economic conditions. But he was emphatically not of that sort, so continued to lead his disreputable, roving life for a period of ten years. At the end of which time he met a plaintive little Englishwoman, just out from Home, and she, knowing nothing whatever of Rivers, but being taken with his glib tongue and rather handsome person, married him.

As the wife of a confirmed beach-comber she had rather a hard time of it. But for all that she was so plaintive and so supine, there was a certain quality of force within her, and she insisted upon some provision for the future. They were living in the interior at that time, not too far in, and Rivers had come down to Shanghai to negotiate some transactions for a certain firm. He could do things like that well enough when he wanted to, as he had a certain ability, and a knowledge of two or three Chinese dialects, and these things he could put to account when he felt like it. Aided by his wife, stimulated by her quiet, subtle insistence, he put through the business entrusted to him, and the business promised success. Which meant that the interior town in which they found themselves would soon be opened to foreign trade. And as a new trade centre, however small, Europeans would come to the town from time to time and require a night's lodging. Here was where Mrs. Rivers saw her chance and took it. In her simple, wholly supine way, she realised that there were nothing but Chinese inns in the place, and therefore it would be a good opportunity to open a hotel for foreigners. Numbers of foreigners would soon be arriving, thanks to Rivers' efforts, and as he was now out of employment (having gone on a prolonged spree to celebrate his success and been discharged in consequence), there still remained an opportunity for helping foreigners in another way. Personally, he would have preferred to open a gambling house, but the risks were too great. At that time the town was not yet fully civilized or Europeanised, and he realised that he

Ellen Newbold La Motte

would encounter considerable opposition to this scheme from the Chinese—and he was without sufficient influence or protection to oppose them. His wife, therefore, insisted upon the hotel, and he saw her point. She did not make it in behalf of her own welfare, or the welfare of possible future children. She merely made it as an opportunity that a man of his parts ought not to miss. He had made a few hundred dollars out of his deal, and fortunately, had not spent all of it on his grand carouse. There was enough left for the new enterprise.

So they took a temple. Buddhism being in a decadent state in China, and the temples being in a still further state of decay, it was an easy matter to arrange things with the priests. The temple selected was a large, rambling affair, with many compounds and many rooms, situated in the heart of the city, and near the newly opened offices of the newly established firm, the nucleus of this coming trade centre of China. A hundred dollars Mex. rented it for a year, and Mrs. Rivers spent many days sweeping and cleaning it, while Rivers himself helped occasionally, and hired several coolies to assist in the work as well. The monks' houses were washed and white-washed; clean, new mats spread on the floors, cheap European cots installed, with wash basins, jugs and chairs, and other accessories such as are not found in native inns. The main part of the temple still remained open for worship, with the dusty gods on the altars and the dingy hangings in place as usual. The faithful, such as there were, still had access to it, and the priests lived in one of the compounds, but all the other compounds were given over to Rivers for his new enterprise. Thus the prejudices of the townspeople were not excited, the old priests cleared a hundred dollars Mex., while the new tenants were at liberty to pursue their venture to its most profitable limits. Mrs. Rivers managed the housekeeping, assisted by a capable Chinese cook, and Rivers had a sign painted, in English, bearing the words "Temple Hotel." Fortunately it was summertime, so there were no expenses for artificial heat, an item which would have taxed their small capital beyond its limits.

Two weeks after the Temple Hotel swung out its sign, the first guest arrived, the manager of the new company. He came to town reluctantly, dreading the discomforts of a Chinese inn, and bringing with him his food and bedding roll, intending to sleep in his cart in the courtyard. Consequently he was greatly pleased and greatly surprised to find a European hotel, and he stayed there ten days in perfect comfort. Mrs. Rivers treated him royally—lost money on him, in fact, but it was a good investment. At parting, the manager told Rivers that his wife was a marvel, as indeed she was. Then he went down to Shanghai and spread the news among his friends, and from that time on, the success of the Temple Hotel was assured. True, Rivers still continued to be a good fellow, that is, he continued to drink pretty hard, but his guests overlooked it and his wife was used to it, and the establishment continued to flourish. In a year or two the railroad came along, and a period of great prosperity set in all round.

Like most foreigners, Rivers had a profound contempt for the Chinese. They were inferior beings, made for servants and underlings, and to serve the dominant race. He was at no pains to conceal this dislike, and backed it up by blows and curses as occasion required. In this he was not alone, however, nor in any way peculiar. Others of his race feel the same contempt for the Chinese and manifest it by similar demonstrations. Lying drunk under a walnut tree of the main courtyard, Rivers had only to raise his eyes to his blue-coated, pig-tailed coolies, to be immensely aware of his superiority. Kwong, his number-one boy, used to survey him thus stretched upon the ground, while Rivers, helpless, would explain to Kwong what deep and profound contempt he felt for all those who had not his advantages—the great, God-given advantage of a white skin. The lower down one is on the social and moral plane, the more necessary to emphasize the distinction between the races. Kwong used to listen, imperturbable, thinking his own thoughts. When his master beat him, he submitted. His impassive face expressed no emotion, neither assent nor dissent.

Ellen Newbold La Motte

Except for incidents like these, of some frequency, things went on very well with Rivers for three or four years, and then something happened. He had barely time to bundle his wife and children aboard an English ship lying in harbour and send them down river to Shanghai, before the revolution broke out. He himself stayed behind to see it through, living in the comparative security of his Consulate, for the outbreak was not directed against foreigners and he was safe enough outside the city, in the newly acquired concession. On this particular day, when things had reached their climax and the rebels were sacking and burning the town, Rivers leaned over the ramparts of the city wall and watched them. The whole Tartar City was in flames, including the Temple Hotel. He watched it burn with satisfaction. When things quieted down, he would put in his claim for an indemnity. The Chinese government, which-ever or whatever it happened to be, should be made to pay handsomely for his loss. Really, at this stage of his fortunes nothing could have been more opportune. The Temple Hotel had reached the limit of its capacity, and he had been obliged to turn away guests. Moreover the priests, shrewd old sinners, had begun to clamour for increased rental. They had detected signs of prosperity—as indeed, who could not detect it—and for some time past they had been urging that a hundred dollars Mex. a year was inadequate compensation. Well, this revolution, whatever it was all about, would put a stop to all that. Rivers would claim, and would undoubtedly receive, an ample indemnity, with which money he would build himself a fine modern hostelry, such as befitted this flourishing new trade centre, and as befitted himself, shrewd and clever man of affairs. Altogether, this revolution was a most timely and fortunate occurrence. He surveyed the scene beneath him, but a good way off, be it said. Shrieks and yells, firing and destruction, and the whole Tartar City in names and fast crumbling into ashes.

The revolution settled itself in due time. The rebels either got what they wanted, or didn't get what they wanted, or changed their minds about wanting it after all, as sometimes happens with Chinese uprisings. Whichever way it was, law and order were finally restored and life resumed itself again on normal lines, although the Tartar City, lying within the Chinese City, was a total wreck. What happened in consequence to the despoiled and dispersed Manchu element is no concern of ours.

Rivers put in his claim for an indemnity and got it. It was awarded promptly, that is, with the delay of only a few months, and he at once set out to build himself a fine hotel, in accordance with his highest ambitions. The construction was entrusted to a native contractor, and while the work progressed apace, he and his wife went down river to Shanghai, and the children were sent north somewhere to a mission school. During this enforced residence in Shanghai, in which city he had been known some years ago as a pronounced beach-comber and ne'er-do-weel, he was obliged to live practically without funds. However, he was able to borrow on the strength of his indemnity, but to do him justice, he limited his borrowings to the lowest terms, not wishing to encroach upon his capital. In all this economy of living, his wife assisted him greatly, for although supine and flexible there was that quality of force about her which we have mentioned before.

As befitted a person who had lost his all in a Chinese uprising and had been rewarded with a large sum of money in return, Rivers was particularly bitter against the Chinese. His old contempt and hatred flared up to large proportions, and he expressed his feelings openly and freely, especially at those times when alcohol clouded his judgment. Moreover, he was living in Shanghai now, where it was easy to express his feelings in the classic way approved by foreigners, and sanctioned by the customs and usages of the International Settlement. He delighted to walk along the Bund, among crowds of burdened coolies bending and panting under great sacks of rice, and to see them shrink and swerve as he approached, fearing a blow of his stick. When he rode in rickshaws, he habitually cheated the coolie of his proper fare, secure in the knowledge that the Chinese had no redress, could appeal to no one, and must accept a few coppers or none at all, at his pleasure. If the coolie objected, Rivers still had the rights of it. A crowd might collect, vociferating in their vile jargon, but it mattered nothing. A word from Rivers to a passing European, to a policeman, to any one whose word carries in the Settlement, was sufficient. He had but to explain that one of these impertinent yellow pigs had tried to extort three times the legal fare, and his case was won. No coolie could successfully contradict the word of a foreigner, no police court, should matters go as far as that, would take a Chinaman's word against that of a white man. He was quite secure in his bullying, in his dishonesty, in his brutality, and there is no place on earth where the white man is more secure in his whitemanishness than in this Settlement, administered by the ruling races of the world. Rivers thoroughly enjoyed these street fracases, in which he was the natural and logical victor. He enjoyed telling about them afterward, for they served to illustrate his conception of the Chinese character and of the Chinese race in general. It was but natural for him to feel this way, seeing what losses he had suffered through the revolution. As he told of his losses, it was not apparent to an outsider that the hotel had not been utterly and entirely his property, instead of an old Buddhist temple rented from the priests for one hundred dollars Mex. a year.

Besides Rivers, others in the town in the interior had suffered hardships. Among them was his number-one boy, Kwong, who had served him faithfully for several years. Kwong had been rather hard hit by the uprising. His wretched little hovel had been burned to the ground, his wife had fallen victim to a bullet, while his two younger children disappeared during the excitement and were never heard of again. Killed, presumably. After the victorious rebels had had their way, all that remained to Kwong was his son Liu, aged eighteen, and these two decided to come down to Shanghai and earn their living amidst more civilized surroundings. One of the strongest arguments in favour of the International Settlement is that it affords safety and protection to the Chinese. They flock to it in great numbers, preferring the just and beneficent administration of the white man to the uncertainties of native rule. So

Kwong and his son made their way down the Yangtzse, floating down river on a stately junk with ragged matting sails. It was the tide, and a bamboo pole for pushing, rather than any assistance derived from the ragged sails, which eventually landed them in the safe harbour of Whangpoo Creek, and stranded them on the mud flats below Garden Bridge.

Being illiterate people, father and son, unskilled labour was all that presented itself, so they became rickshaw coolies, as so many country people do. During a year, some two hundred thousand men, young and old and mostly from up-country, take up the work of rickshaw runners. It is not profitable employment, and the work is hard, and many of them drop out—the come-and-go of rickshaw runners is enormous, a great, unstable, floating population. Kwong and Liu hired a rickshaw between them, for a dollar and ten cents a day, and their united exertions barely covered the day's hire. Sometimes they had a few coppers over and above the daily expenses, sometimes they fell below that sum and had to make up the deficit on the morrow. On the occasions when they were in debt to the proprietor, they were forced to forego the small outlay required for food, and neither could afford a meagre bowl of millet. Pulling a rickshaw on an empty stomach is not conducive to health. Kwong, being an older man, found the strain very difficult, and Liu, being but a fledgling and weak and undeveloped at that, also found it difficult. They were always tired, nearly always hungry, and part of the time ill. And what neither could understand was the passengers' objection to paying the legal fare. Now and then, of course, they had a windfall in the shape of a tourist or a drunken sailor from a cruiser, but these exceptions were few and far between. Necessarily so, considering the number of rickshaws, and that the tram cars were strong competitors as well.

They were also surprised at the attitude of the Europeans. The first time that Liu was struck over the head by a beautiful Malacca cane, he was aghast with astonishment—and pain. Fortunately he knew enough not to hit hack. Not understanding English, he did not know that he was being directed to turn up the Peking Road, and accordingly had run swiftly past the Peking Road until brought to his senses, so to speak, by a silver knob above the ear, which made him dizzy with pain. As time passed, however, he grew accustomed to this attitude of the ruling race, and accepted the blows without remonstrance, knowing that remonstrance was vain. His fellow coolies soon taught him that. He and his kind were but dogs in the sight of the foreigners, and must accept a dog's treatment in consequence. Once a lady leaned far forward in the rickshaw and gave him a vicious kick. Up till then, he had not realised that the women of the white race also had this same feeling towards him. But what can one expect? If a man lowers himself to the plane of an animal and gets between shafts, he must expect an animal's treatment. In certain communities, however, there are societies to protect animals.

Matters went along like this for some months, and Kwong and Liu barely kept themselves going. However, they managed to keep out of debt for the rickshaw hire, which was in itself an achievement. Rivers also continued to live in Shanghai at this time, making up-river trips now and then to inspect the progress of his new hotel, which was favourable. As he landed at the Bund one day, returning from one of these excursions, he chanced to step into the rickshaw pulled by his old servitor, Kwong. Kwong made him a respectful salute, but Rivers, preoccupied, failed to recognise his former servant in the old and filthy coolie who stood between the shafts of an old and shabby rickshaw. He always made it a point to select old rickshaws, pulled by broken down men. They looked habit-ually underpaid, and were probably used to it, and were therefore less likely to raise objections at the end of the trip than one of the swift young runners who stood about the European hotels. Remember, in extenuation, that Rivers was living on credit at this time, on borrowed money, and he did not like to be more extravagant than he had to.

The day was a piping hot one, and the distance Rivers travelled was something under three miles, out on the edge of French Town. When he alighted, he found but three copper cents in his pocket, all that was left him after a considerable carouse on the river boat coming down. He tendered this sum to the panting and sweating Kwong, who stood exhausted but respectful, hoping in a friendly way that his old master would recognise him. To do Rivers justice, he did not recognise his former servant, nor did he have more than three copper cents in his possession, although that fact was known to him when he stepped into the rickshaw and directed the coolie to French Town, extreme limits. Kwong indignantly rejected the copper cents, and Rivers flung them into the dust and turned away. Kwong ran after him, expostulating, catching him by the coat sleeve. Rivers turned savagely. The wide road was deserted, and in a flash he brought his heavy blackwood stick across Kwong's face with a terrific blow. The coolie fell sprawling in the dust at his old master's feet, and Rivers, furious, kicked him savagely in the stomach, again and again, until the man lay still and ceased writhing. Blood gushed from his mouth, making a puddle in the dust, a puddle which turned black and thick about the edges.

In an instant Rivers was sobered. He glanced swiftly up and down the road, and to his dismay, saw a crowd of blue coated figures running in his direction. He had barely time to stoop down and pick up the tell-tale coppers before he was surrounded by a noisy and excited group of Chinese, gesticulating furiously and rending the hot, blue air with their outlandish cries. A policeman came in sight, and a passing motor filled with foreigners stopped to see the trouble. He had overdone things, surely. There was nothing for it but the police station.

Now such accidents are not infrequent in Shanghai, the white man's city built in China, administered by the white men to their own advantage, and to the advantage of the Chinese who seek protection under the white man's just and beneficent rule. However, human life is very cheap in China, cheaper than most places in the Orient, although that is not saying much. It would, therefore, have been very easy for Rivers to have extricated himself from this scrape had he possessed any

Ellen Newbold La Motte

money. Two hundred and fifty dollars, Mex. is the usual price for a coolie's life when an affair of this kind happens. There is a well established precedent to this effect. Unfortunately for Rivers, he did not possess two hundred and fifty dollars, for as has been said, he was at this time living on borrowed money. Nothing for it then but a trial, and certain unpleasant publicity. Happily, there were no witnesses to the occurrence, and Rivers' plea of self-defence would naturally he accepted. It was an unpleasant business, however, but there was no other way out of it, seeing that he was bankrupt.

The trial took place with due dignity. Evidence, produced after an autopsy, proved that at the time of the accident Kwong was in a very poor state of health. Every one knows that the work of a rickshaw coolie is hard, the physical strain exceedingly severe. Four years, at the outside, is the average life of a rickshaw runner, after which he must change his occupation to something more suited to a physical wreck. Much testimony was produced to show that Kwong had long ago reached that point. He was courting death, defying death, every day. It was his own fault. He had great varicose veins in his legs, which were large and swollen. His heart, constantly overtaxed by running with heavy weights, was enlarged and ready to burst any moment. His spleen also was greatly dilated and ready to burst—in fact, it was not at all clear whether after such a long run—three miles in such heat—he would not have dropped dead anyway. Such cases were of daily occurrence, too numerous to mention. The slight blow he had received—a mere push as defendant had stated under oath—was probably nothing more than a mere unfortunate coincidence.

Such being the evidence, and the courts being administered by Europeans, and there being no doubt whatever of the quality of justice administered by Europeans in their own behalf, it is not surprising that Rivers was acquitted. The verdict returned was, Accidental death due to rupture of the spleen, caused by over-exertion. Rivers was a good deal shaken, however, when he stepped out of the courtroom, into the hot, bright sunshine, and received the congratulations of his friends. He had heard so many disgusting medical details of the havoc caused by rickshaw pulling, that he resolved to be very careful in future about hitting these impudent, good-for-nothing swine.

Amongst the crowd in the courtroom, but practically unnoticed, sat Liu, son of the late Kwong. The proceedings being in English, he was unable to follow them, but he knew enough to realise that the slayer of his father was being tried. Presumably his life was at stake, as was befitting under the circumstances. Therefore his surprise was great when the outcome of the case was explained to him by a Chinese friend who understood English, and his astonishment, if such it may be called, was still more intense upon seeing Rivers walk out of the courtroom receiving congratulatory handshakes as he passed. To the ignorant mind of the young Chinese, Rivers was being felicitated for having committed murder. He was unable to draw any fine distinctions, or to understand that these congratulations were not intended for Rivers personally, but because his acquittal strengthened established precedents. Precedents that rendered unassailable the status of the ruling race. Liu was therefore filled with an overmastering and bitter hatred of Rivers, and had he realised what the acquittal stood for, would probably have been filled with an equally intense hatred for the dominant race in general. Not understanding that, however, he concentrated his feelings upon Rivers, and resolved to bring him to account in accord with simpler, less civilized standards.

Within two months, the Temple Hotel was finished and ready for use. Much foreign furniture had been sent up from Shanghai, and Rivers and his wife also removed themselves to the up-river town and set about their business. Rivers was glad to leave Shanghai; he had had enough of it, since his unlucky episode, and was glad to bury himself in the comparative obscurity of the interior. Life resumed itself smoothly once again, and he prospered exceedingly.

His attitude towards the natives, however, was more domineering than ever, now that he had recovered from the unpleasant two weeks that preceded his trial. These two weeks had been more uncomfortable than he liked to think about, but safely away from the scene of the disturbance, he became more abusive, more brutal than ever in his attitude towards the Chinese. His servants horribly feared him, yet did his bidding with alacrity. The reputation of a man who could kill when he chose, with impunity, stood him in good stead. Liu, the son of Kwong, followed him up-river and obtained a place in his household as pidgeon-cook, assistant to number-one cook. Rivers failed to recognize his new servant, and at such times as he encountered him, was delighted with the servile attitude of the youth, and called him "Son of a Turtle" which is the worst insult in the Chinese language.

Liu bided his time, for time is of no moment in the Orient. His hatred grew from day to day, but he continued to wait. He wished to see Rivers thoroughly successful, at the height of his career, before calling him to account. Since he would have to pay for his revenge with his life—not being a European—he determined that a white man at the top of his pride would be a more fitting victim than one who had not yet climbed the ladder. Such was his simple reasoning. Under his long blue coat there hung a long, thin knife, whetted to razor sharpness on both edges.

Summer came again, and the blazing heat of mid-China, lay over the land. Mrs. Rivers went north to join her children, and the number of guests in the hotel diminished to two or three. Business and tourists came to a standstill during these scorching weeks, and Rivers finally went down to Shanghai for a few days' jollification. He left his affairs in the hands of the shroff, the Chinese accountant, who could be trusted to manage them for a short time.

He returned unexpectedly one night about eleven o'clock, quite drunk. The few guests had retired and the hotel was closed. At the gate, the watchman lay asleep beside his lantern, and when Rivers let himself in with his key, he found Liu in the lounge, also asleep. He cursed Liu, but submitted to the steady, supporting arm which the boy place around his waist, and was led to bed without difficulty. Liu assisted his master to undress, folding up the crumpled, white linen clothes with silver buttons, and laying them neatly across a chair. He was an excellent servant. Then he retired from the room, listening outside the door till he heard sounds of heavy, stertorous breathing. At that moment, the contempt of the Chinese for the dominant race was even greater than Rivers' contempt for the inferior one.

When the proprietor's breathing had assumed reassuring proportions, Liu opened the door cautiously, and stepped lightly into the room. He then locked it with equal caution, slipped quietly across to the verandah, and passed out through the long, wide-open windows. The verandah was a dozen feet from the ground, and the dark passage below, leading to the gate, was deserted. At the other end sat the watchman with his lantern, presumably asleep. Liu had not heard his drum tap for an hour. A shaft of moonlight penetrated the room, and a light wind blowing in from outside gently stirred the mosquito curtains over the bed. Liu tiptoed to the bed, and with infinite care drew the netting aside and stood surveying his victim. Rivers lay quite still with arms outstretched, fat and bloated, breathing with hoarse, blowing sounds, quite repulsive. The moonlight was sufficient to enable Liu to see the dark outline upon the bed, and to gauge where he would strike. He hovered over his victim, exultant, prolonging from minute to minute this strange, new feeling of power and dominance. That was what it meant to be a white man—to feel this feeling always— always—all one's life, not merely for a few brief, exhilarating moments! And with that feeling of power and dominance was the ability to inflict pain, horrible, frightful pain. That also was part of the white man's heritage, this ability to inflict pain and suffering at will. And after that, death. Liu also had the power to inflict death. Leaning over the bed, with the long, keen knife in his steady clutch, he was for those glorious moments the equal of the white man! He prolonged his sensations breathlessly—this sense of superb power, this superb ability to inflict humiliation, pain and death.

Ellen Newbold La Motte

A mosquito lit on Rivers' blotched cheek, and he raised a heavy arm to brush it away. Then he relaxed again with a snore. Liu paused, waiting. The glorious exaltation was mounting higher. It occurred to him to sharpen these sensations, to heighten them. After all, he was about to kill a drunken man in a drunken sleep. He wanted something better. He wanted to feel his power over a conscious man, a man conscious and aware of what was to befall him. Even as his father had been conscious and aware of what was befalling him, even as thousands of his countrymen were awake and aware, knowing what was being done to them—by the dominant race. He wished Rivers awake and aware. It involved greater risk, but it was worth it. Therefore, with the point of his sharp, keen knife, he gently prodded the throat of the sleeper, lying supine before him under the moon rays. Gently, very gently, he prodded the exposed throat, placed the point of his knife very gently upon his heaving, corded larynx, which pulsed inward and outward under the heaving, stertorous breaths. Gently he stimulated the corded, puffing throat, gently, with the point of his sharp knife.

The result was as he wished. First Rivers stirred, moved a restless arm, flopped an impotent, heavy arm that fell back upon the pillow, an arm that failed to reach its objective, to quell the tickling, cold point prodded into his throat. Then as he slowly grew conscious, the movements of the arm became more coordinated. Into his drunken mind came the fixed sensation of a disturbance at his throat. He became conscious, opened a heavy eye, and fixed it upon Liu, without at the same time feeling the pressing point at his throat. Liu saw his returning consciousness, and leaning over him, pressed upon his throat, ever so lightly, the point of his long knife. Thus for a moment or two they regarded each other, Liu having the advantage. But so it had always been. Having the advantage was one of the attributes of the dominant race. Thus for those few brief seconds, Liu experienced the whole glory of it. And as little by little Rivers emerged from the drunken to the conscious, to the abjectly, cravenly conscious, so Liu mounted to the heights.

Then he saw that Rivers was about to cry out. To let forth a roaring bellow, a howling bellow. Enough. He had tasted the whole of it. He had felt, for prolonged and glorious moments, the feelings of the superior race. Therefore he drove home, silently, his sharp, keen knife, and stifled the mad bellow that was about to be let forth. After which, he crept very cautiously to the balcony, and peered anxiously up and down the dark alleyway beneath. He lowered himself with infinite caution over the railing. He had become once more the cringing Oriental.

Ellen Newbold La Motte

HOMESICK

A Chinese gentleman, with his arms tucked up inside the brocaded sleeves of his satin coat, stood one day with one foot in China and the other upon European soil. From time to time he bore with alternate weight upon the right foot, on Chinese soil, and then upon the left foot, upon European soil, and his mental attitude shifted from right to left accordingly. The foot upon Chinese soil reflected upward to his brain the restriction of Chinese laws, the breaking of which were accompanied by heavy penalties. The foot upon European soil reassured him as to his ability to indulge himself, with no penalties whatsoever. Therefore, after balancing himself for a few moments first upon this foot, then upon that, he gave way to his inclinations and resolved to indulge them. In certain matters, Europeans were more liberal than Chinese.

From this you will see that he had been standing with one foot in China, where opium traffic was prohibited, where heavy fines were attached to opium smoking and to opium buying, where heavy jail sentences were imposed upon those who smoked or bought opium, while the other foot, planted upon the ground of the Foreign Concession, assured him of his absolute freedom to buy opium in any quantity he chose, and to smoke himself to a standstill in an opium den licensed under European auspices. In his saner moments, when not under the influence of the drug, he resented the European occupation of certain parts of Chinese territory, but when his craving for opium occurred—which it did with great frequency—he was delighted to realise that there were certain parts of China not under the authorityof the drastic laws of China, which laws prohibited with such drastic and heavy penalties the indulgences he craved. Therefore he swayed himself backwards and forwards for a space, first upon this foot, then upon that, and finally withdrew both feet into the Foreign Concession, and directed his steps to a shop where opium was sold under European influence. The shop was capacious but dark. He stated his requirements and they were measured out to him—a large keg was withdrawn from its place on a shelf, and a gentle Chinese, clad, like himself, in satin brocade, dug into the contents of the keg with a ladle and withdrew from it a black, molasses-like substance, which ran slowly and gummily from the ladle into the small silver box which the customer had produced. The box finally filled, with some of the gummy, black contents running over the edges, our gentleman withdrew himself, having accomplished his purpose. Tucked into the security of his belt, it was impossible to detect the contraband as he again stepped over the boundary line which separated Chinese from European soil.

Half an hour after our Chinese gentleman had stepped across the boundary line into the native city, with a large supply of opium concealed in his belt, part of which he would retail to certain friends who had not time enough to run across into the European concession to buy it for themselves, a young Englishman stood, by curious coincidence, upon the same spot recently occupied by the Chinese. He also stood with one foot upon Chinese soil, with the other upon the soil of the Foreign Concession, and regretted, with considerable vehemence, that at this dividing line his efforts must cease. He had been pursuing, for perhaps a mile, the proprietor of a certain gambling den, whom he wished to apprehend. But at the boundary line, which the Chinese had reached before him, his prey had escaped. He was off somewhere, safe in the devious lanes and burrows of the native city. Therefore he stood baffled, and finally made his way back into the Settlement, along the quais, and finally reached his rooms. He pondered somewhat over the situation. That which was permitted on Chinese territory, was prohibited in the foreign holdings—and the reverse. It just depended whether you were on this side the line or that, as to whether or not you were a lawbreaker. Morality appeared arbitrary, determined by geographical lines—a matter of dollars and cents. Lawson walked slowly along the Bund, turning the matter over in his rather limited mind. Take the opium business, he considered. The Chinese considered it harmful, and wished to abolish it. Very good. Yet the Foreign Concessions made money out of it and insisted upon selling it.

Take another example, he reflected—gambling, his job. Or rather, his job was the suppression of gambling—in the foreign holdings. The Chinese considered it harmless, a matter of individual inclination. Very good. But the foreigners considered it a vice, and he, Lawson, was appointed to run to earth Chinese fan-tan houses, in the Concession, and suppress them. Yet his own people, the foreigners, gambled freely and uproariously in their own establishments—at the races, and at certain houses which they maintained for their pleasure. True, these houses were not in the Concession—for some reason the foreigners had set their face against gambling in the Concession—yet they maintained their establishments, their showy and luxurious establishments, outside the Concession and upon Chinese soil. They must pay a handsome squeeze for the privilege. Yet it was difficult to reconcile. What was right and wrong, anyway? What was moral or immoral, anyway? Lawson, of very limited intelligence, walked along, sorely puzzled. Sauce for the goose, sauce for the gander—well, two very different kinds of sauces, composed of very different ingredients, as far as he could see. Lawson, being a young man of limited intelligence, was greatly puzzled. He had been greatly bothered over this for a long time. It began to look to him—very vaguely—as if morality was not an abstract but a concrete affair.

Just then he passed an opium shop, and considered again. That surely was a nasty game, yet his Government encouraged it—and made money from it. But the Chinese, on their side of the boundary line, were doing their best to suppress it. It was very difficult for them to make headway, however, since opium shops flourished and were encouraged by the foreign concessions, over which the Chinese had no control. Topsy turvy, anyway. No wonder a person like Lawson was unable to understand it. It all resolved itself into a question of money, after all. For after all, money was the main object of life, whether on the part of an individual or of a government. And since all governments were composed of individuals, and reflected the ideas of individuals, there you were!

By this time, young Lawson had become quite bored with life in the Far East. The romance was gone and it offered so little variety. One day was so like another, and every day, winter and summer, it was the same thing or the same sorts of things, and there was an intense sameness about it all. By day he did his work—that goes without saying—one has to work in the Far East, that is what one comes out to do. Otherwise, why come? Unless one is a tourist or a missionary, or a buyer of Chinese antiques, or has had an overwhelming desire to write a book upon international politics, a desire springing from the depths of gross ignorance. But after all, why not such a book? It reaches, if it reaches at all, a public still less informed, and misinformation is as valuable as no information at all, when we desire to interfere with the destiny of the Chinese. In his leisure moments, Lawson had tried his hand at such a book— until he suddenly realised that he had been in the Orient too long to make it a success. He knew just a trifle too much about affairs, and found himself setting forth facts which would lead to his undoing, as a minor official in the International Settlement—if he gave them publicity. He could not afford to lose his position. And he was by no means sure that the deep, unerring sense of justice, the innate instinct of the masses, would rally to his support. He had his own opinion of the ruling classes, but he trusted the masses still less.

It was a biting cold night, with a high wind from the north howling down the long streets and whipping the waters of the harbour into a fury. Junks strained at their anchors, tossed and heaved, and now and then one broke loose from its moorings and wandered about adrift, spreading infinite terror amongst the owners of other junks, who feared for their safety. A cruiser or two lay in the roads, and the French mail, and two or three Japanese cargo-boats, and half a dozen tramp ships from the China Coast, but none of these were unduly buffeted by the gale, which only created havoc among the junks and sampans. Lawson's lodgings overlooked the harbour, and he laid down his pen and moved from the table to the dark window, trying in vain to see what was going on without. Below, the long line of the quais was outlined by long rows of electric lights, swaying and tossing from their poles, and illuminating the shining, wet asphalt of the Bund. He was very, very tired of it all. So many years he had been out, and the same monotonous round must be gone through with, over and over again, day after day—until he made money enough to return home. And as a salaried clerk, a court runner, whose duty it was to enforce the laws against gambling in the Settlement, that day seemed very far distant indeed. Whenever he heard of a fan-tan place—and he heard of them every day—he must investigate, see that it was closed and the keepers, if he was lucky enough to catch them, duly punished. And the players as well. Now to eradicate gambling from amongst the Chinese is a difficult task, futile and ridiculous, a good waste of time and money. He wondered why his Government should attempt it. Foolish thing for his Government to do—yet what would become of Lawson if the undertaking were abolished? Taste tea, probably—apprentice himself to some tea merchant, and learn all the nasty role of tea spitting. From which you will see that Lawson was squeamish about some things, and did not envy those of his friends who had become tea tasters, and who moved all day up and down a long table, filled with rows of stupid little cups, with an attendant China boy forever shoving a cuspidor from one advanced position to another. And if not a tea taster, then some commercial house would absorb his energies, which would be worse still—close at his elbow a spectacled Chinese clicking all day upon a dirty little abacus, —checking him up, keeping tabs on him.

No, the work he had was better. But he was so tired of it. He leaned himself against the dripping, cold pane, and regarded the lights below, shining on the wet asphalt of the quais. He was thirty years old and ten years in the East had about done for him. The East does, for many people. Yes, he reflected bitterly, it had about done for him. It undermines people, in some mysterious manner, and in Lawson's case there had been so little to undermine. He had little imagination, and could never imagine the larger possibilities of life, and what he had missed, therefore the undermining of his character was of small account. He was only conscious of an intense boredom, and to-night the boredom was accentuated, because of the weather. He was too inert to splash about in such a driving rain in quest of a friend more weary than himself.

If he could just get out of it all! By which, understand, he had not the adventurous spirit of the beach-comber, the adventurer who combs pleasure and profits from the ports of the China Coast. He wasn't that sort. He had no desire to take a sampan and row out to the nearest cargo-boat and ship away to the Southern Seas, and sink himself in romance north or south of the Line. No, the mystery of the East, the romance of foreign lands made no appeal to him. And the everlasting monotony of his daily work, of his daily association with his few wearied friends, clerks and suchlike, all minor and unimportant cogs of the big machine overseas, offered him nothing. Very decidedly he was homesick. But his tired mind came upon a blank wall—he had no home to be homesick for. Nothing compelling, nothing to return to—all broken up long ago, such as it was, long before he had come out to the Orient. Yet he was longing for the sight of his native land again. Yes, that was it—just the familiar sight of it. It offered him nothing in the way of tie or kin, yet he was longing to see it again, just his own native land. He was exiled in China—and he was exiled at Home, when you got down to it—but to-night his home land drew him with overwhelming insistence.

What can you do, I'd like to know, when you are like this? Along the outskirts of the Settlement stood big houses, cheerful with lights, with home life, with all that the successful ones had brought out from Home, to establish Home in the Orient. But Lawson had nothing to do with these, with all the pompous, successful ones, who ignored him completely and were unaware of his existence. They were all superior to him, with the superiority that new-found money brings, and they looked down upon him as a cheap court runner, told off to round up the fan-tan playing Chinese. You see, Lawson was common—he had sprung from nothing and was nothing. But these others, these successful ones, they too had sprung from nothing, but out here in the Orient they had become important. Through the possession of certain qualities which Lawson did not possess, they had become large and prominent in the community. They referred to themselves, among each other, as "younger sons." Which left one to infer that they were of distinguished lineage. But Lawson knew better, and knew it with great bitterness. Like himself, they were indeed "younger sons"—of greengrocers. Therefore, for that reason perhaps, they went home seldom, for at home they were nobodies. Whereas out here—oh, out here, by reason of certain qualities which Lawson did not possess, they were important and pompous, and lived in big houses, with lights and guests and servants and motors. Therefore Lawson resented them, because they thought he was common. And he was common, he admitted bitterly, but so were they. Only they were successful, by reason of certain qualities which he did not possess. They ignored him, and left him alone in the community, and it is never very good to be too much alone, especially in the Far East. True, they provided him with his job—with his wretchedly paid little Government job, which they maintained for no altruistic or moral reasons. To suppress gambling amongst the Chinese? Perhaps. Incidentally, on the surface, it looked well. Looked well, he considered, coming from those who never helped the Chinese in anything else. Who exploited them, in all possible ways, and undermined them—undermined the Chinese who were pretty well done for anyway, by nature, being Chinese. No, he reflected savagely—he had heard the story—one night some big personage living in one of the big houses, to which he was never invited—had given a big dinner, with much wine and fine food and many guests and all the rest of it—and what happened? No servants, or rather many servants without liveries or clothing of any kind, everything having been pawned the evening before over the fan-tan tables. Therefore he, Lawson, was employed by Government to suppress these gambling houses, to keep the servants from stealing and pawning their liveries, making embarrassment in the big, foreign-style houses, making amusement and consternation and scandal. He had happened along shortly after this affair, and so obtained the appointment.

Lawson leaned his forehead against the cold glass, down which the rain poured in sheets. The lights of the French mail glimmered intermittently through the darkness—to-morrow she would weigh anchor and be off for Marseilles, for Home. Not that he had a home, as we have said, but he longed for the familiar look of things, for the crowds all speaking his own tongue, for the places he knew, th e wellknown street signs, and the big hoardings. And he couldn't go back. Hehad not money enough to go back. Every penny of his little salary went for living expenses and living comes high in China. To say nothing of the passage money and the money for afterwards— A gentle cough behind him made him turn round in a hurry. His China-boy stood expectantly in the doorway.

"What is it?" demanded Lawson sharply. Ah Chang drew in his breath, not wishing to breathe upon his superior. The indrawn, hissing noise irritated Lawson immensely. He had been out ten years, and in that time had never learned that Ah Chang and the others were showing him respect, deep proofs of Oriental respect, when they sucked in their breath with that hissing noise, to avoid breathing upon a superior. To Lawson it was just another horrid trait, another horrid native characteristic.

"Man come see Master," observed Ah Chang, addressing space impersonally. "Heap plenty important business. You see?"

Anything for a change this dreary evening. "Very well," said Lawson, "I see." In a moment or two, a tall Chinese shuffled into the room, bowing repeatedly with hands on knees. After which he passed his long slim hands up into the sleeves of his satin coat, and waited quietly till the boy withdrew. He gave a swift look about the room, a glance so hurried that it seemed impossible he could have satisfied himself that they were alone, and then began to speak. Lawson recognised him at once as the keeper of a house he had raided the week before, a big, crowded place, where the police had captured a score of players and much money. It was an important haul, a notorious den, that they had been after for a long time. Only it changed its location so often, moved from place to place each night, or so it seemed, that Lawson had spent months trying to find it. It is not easy finding such places in the crowded, native streets of the Concession, and he had stumbled upon it by a piece of sheer luck. And the proprietor had been heavily fined and heavily warned, yet here he stood to-night, silent, respectful, hands up his sleeves, waiting. For once in his life, Lawson's imagination worked. He foresaw something portentous looming in the background of that impenetrable mind, revealed in the steady, unblinking stare of those slanting Chinese eyes, fixed steadily and fearlessly and patiently upon his.

"Sit down," he commanded, with a sweep of his hand towards an upright chair.

*   *   *   *   *

After his visitor had departed, Lawson stood lost in thought. He was not angry, yet he should have been, he realised. Assuredly he should have been angry, assuredly he should have kicked his visitor downstairs. But as it was, he remained in deep thought, pondering over a suggestion that had been made to him. The suggestion, stripped of certain Oriental qualities of flowery phraseology and translated from pidgin-English into business English, was the merest, most vague hint of an exchange of favours. So slight was the hint, but so overwhelming the possibilities suggested, that, as we have said, Lawson had not kicked his visitor downstairs, but remained standing lost in thought for several moments after his departure. As he had stood earlier in the day, with one foot in the Foreign Concession, and the other on Chinese soil, considering the different standards that obtained in each, so he stood now, figuratively, on the boundary line of an ethical problem and swayed mentally first towards one side and then the other. The irony of it, the humour of it, appealed to him. It seemed so insanely just—just what you might expect. He had been asked—that was too definite a word—to forego his activities for a few brief weeks. And during those few brief weeks he could repay himself, week by week, on Friday nights—

He had been merely asked—too strong a word—the suggestion had been merely hinted at—he balanced himself back and forth over the problem. If his efforts during the next few weeks should prove fruitless, possible enough, considering the wily race he was dealing with—And in exchange, well, once a week on Friday night, he could slip outside the boundaries of the Concession to a large, foreign gambling house kept by and for his own people. By his own people, the Europeans, who employed him to eradicate gambling from amongst the Chinese. Do you wonder that he shifted himself back and forth, morally, first from this point of view, then to that? His own people who objected to gaming, when it involved the loss of their servants' liveries. But they had no such scruples when it came to their own pleasure. Therefore, for their own pleasure, careless of the inconsistency, they had established a very fine place of their own just outside the boundaries of the foreign Concession. Lawson had heard of the place before— the most famous, the most notorious on the China Coast. Kept by the son of a parson, so he had been told, a University graduate. Once, ten years ago, he had gone there and lost a month's pay in an evening. But now it was to be different. He could go there now, every Friday night, and reap the reward of his inability to discover Chinese dens within the Concession.

For nearly an hour he remained undecided, then determined to test the offer made him—but offer was too strong a word. And his salary was so meagre, so abominably small. And the people in the big houses would have none of him, they never invited him, he was left so alone, to himself. He was intensely homesick. Therefore, still on the boundary line, he went to the telephone and called up a certain number. In a confident manner he asked for a limousine. After which he got into his overcoat, muffled himself up well around the ears and nose, for the air outside was cold with a biting north wind, and the rain still drove slantwise in torrents. In a few moments Ah Chang announced that the calliage had come.

Round the earner from his lodgings on a side street and in darkness, stood a big car with the motor puffing violently. It was a big, handsome car, very long, and on the front seat sat two men in livery, one of whom jumped down briskly to open the door. Lawson entered and sank down into the soft cushions, for it was very luxurious. Then the car moved on briskly, without any directions from himself, and he leaned back upon the cushions and took pleasure in the luxury of it, and of the two men in livery upon the front seat, and enjoyed the pouring rain which dashed upon the glass, yet left him so dry and comfortable within. "They will only think it's inconsistent—that's all," he said to himself, "if they ever find out—which is unlikely."

Beyond the confines of the Settlement the motor rapidly made its way, slipping noiselessly over the smooth, wet asphalt, and then out along the bumpy roads beyond the city limits. All was dark now, the street lamps having been left behind with the ending of the good roads, and the car jolted along slowly, over deep ruts. A stretch of open country intervened between the Settlement and a native village of clustering mud huts. Lawson, having no imagination, was not impressed with his position. People did all sorts of things in China, just as elsewhere—only here, in China, it was so much easier to get away with it. His coming to-night might be considered inconsistent, he repeated over and over to himself, but nothing more. Every one did it, he reassured himself.

The car stopped finally, before a pair of high, very solid black gates, and the footman jumped off the box to open the door. He was conscious of a small grill with a yellow face peeping out, backed by flickering lantern light, of a rainy, windswept compound, with a shaft of light from an open door flooding the courtyard. Then he was inside a warm, bright anteroom, with an obsequious China-boy relieving him of overcoat and muffler, and he became aware of many big, fur-lined overcoats, hanging on pegs on the wall. Beyond, in the adjoining room, were two long tables, the players seated with their backs to him, absorbed. Only a few people were present, for the night was early. There was no one there he knew—even had there been, he would not have cared. He drew out a chair and seated himself confidently, while a China-boy pushed a box of cigars towards him, a very good brand. And behind came another boy with a tray of whisky and soda, while a third boy carried sandwiches. It was all very well done, he thought absently. The proprietor, being a parson's son and a University graduate, did it very well. There was no disorder, it was all beautifully done. He wondered what amount of squeeze the Chinese received, for allowing such a fine place to remain undisturbed on Chinese soil. A very big squeeze, certainly. They would surely be very grasping, considering the warfare waged against them, upon their own establishments, by the Europeans. It was all very interesting. Lawson considered the matter critically, from various angles, knowing what he knew. He sorted his chips carefully. It must pay the parson's son well, he concluded, to be able to run such a fine place, in such style, with so much to eat and drink and all, and with all those motors to carry out the guests. All this in addition to the squeeze—it must really be an enormous squeeze. And the people for whose amusement this was established, were the people who were employing him—

For a brief, fleeting second his eye rested upon the calm, unquestioning face of the Chinese at the wheel, brother of the proprietor of the fan-tan place he had raided a week ago. The placid eye of the Oriental fixed his for the fraction of a second, even as he called out the winning numbers. There was no recognition either way, yet Lawson felt himself flushing. The

Ellen Newbold La Motte

wheel spun again and slowly stopped, and he found himself gathering in thirty-five chips, raking them in with eager fingers over the green cloth. It was all right then, after all!

*   *   *   *   *

Lawson was going home. Speaking about this, some said, Well enough—he has become quite incompetent of late. Getting stale, probably. Unable to discover the obvious, losing his keenness. Ten years in the Far East about does for one. But with Lawson, the situation was different. He had become so tired of boundary lines, of perpetual swaying back and forth from one side to the other, without conviction. Geographical and moral concessions, wrong here, right there, had blurred his sense of the abstract. All he was conscious of was an overwhelming desire to leave it all and go home. And now he was going home. He was very glad. It hurt to be so glad. He was going away from China, forever. He was going back to his own land, where he was born, where he belonged, even though there was no one to welcome his return. There was no roof to receive him save an attic roof, rented for a few shillings a week. For though he had plenty of money now, he still thought in small sums. He was glad to be going home—the joy was painful. His chief praised him a little at parting, and said he had done good work and hoped his successor would do as well. Regretted his departure at this moment, since that old fellow who kept such a notorious den was breaking loose again, more villainous, more elusive than ever. Lawson heard this with astonishment, with infinite regret. Wished he could have stayed to see it ended.

He was going home. It hurt to be so glad. In all these years he had been so utterly lonely, so utterly miserable. His few companions came down to the landing stage on the Bund to see him off, to wish him luck. They were rather wistful, for they also knew loneliness. They had tried to forget about this longing for home in the many ways of forgetfulness that the East offered, nevertheless they were wistful. Lawson understood, he felt great pity for them. He advised them to get away before they were done for, for the East does for many people in the long run. The launch, waiting to take him down river where the steamer lay anchored, grated against the steps of the landing stage, as if eager to be off.

"I wish," said one of his friends, "that we had your luck—that we too were going home."

Lawson's heart ached for them. He had experience but no imagination. "Yes," he said simply, "it is very good to be going Home."

CIVILIZATION

I

Maubert leaned against the counter in his wine-shop, reading a paper that had just come to him—an official looking paper, which he held unsteadily, unwillingly, and which trembled a little between his big, thick fingers. Behind the counter sat Madame Maubert, knitting. Before her, ranged neatly on the zinc covered shelf, was a row of inverted wine glasses, three of them still dripping, having been washed after the last customers by a hasty dip into a bucket of cold water.

"Mobilised," said Maubert slowly. "I am mobilised—at last." Madame Maubert looked up from her knitting. For a year now they had both been expecting this, for the war had been going on for over a year, and Maubert, while over age and below par in physical condition, was still a man and as such likely to be called into the reserves. The two exchanged glances.

"When?" asked Madame Maubert, resuming her clicking.

"At once, imbecile," replied her husband stolidly. "Naturally," he continued, "when one is at last sent for, there can be no delay. I must report at once."

"Oh, la la," said Madame Maubert, noncommittally.

Maubert glanced round his shop, his little wine-shop, his

lucrativelittle business that he had made successful. Very well. His wife must run it alone now, as best she could. As best she could, that was evident. She could do many things well. She must do it now while he went forth into service of some kind—into a munition factory probably, or perhaps near the front, as orderly to an officer, or as sentinel, perhaps, along some road in the First Zone of the Armies. He would not be placed on active service—he was too old for that. Nevertheless it meant a horrid jarring out of his usual routine of life, consequently he was angry and resentful, and there was no fine glow of pride or patriotism or such-like feeling in his breast. Bah! All that sort of thing had vanished from men long and long ago, after the first few bitter weeks of war and of realisation of the meaning of war. War was now an affair—a sordid, ugly affair, and Maubert knew it as well as any man. Living in his backwater of a village, keeper of the principal wine-shop of the village, his zinc counter rang every night under emphatic fists, emphasising emphatic remarks about the war, and the remarks were true but devoid of romance. They differed considerably from the tone of the daily press.

From the kitchen beyond came the clattering of dishes, and some talking in immature, childish voices, and the insistent, piping tones of a quite young child. They were all in there, all four of them, the eldest twelve, the youngest four, and Maubert and his wife leaned across the zinc counter and looked at each other.

"It is your fault," he said slowly, with conviction. His eyes, deep set, ugly, sunken, glared angrily into hers. "It is your fault that I am mobilised."

She sat still, rather bewildered, gazing at him steadily. "You wished it!" he began again, "You coward! You trembling coward!"

Still Madame Maubert made no sign, waiting further explanations. She laid down her knitting and took her elbows in her hands, and by gripping her elbows firmly, stopped the

　　　　　Ellen Newbold La Motte

trembling he spoke of.

"You don't understand, eh?" he went on sneeringly. "Always thinking of yourself, of your pretty figure, how to keep yourself always here at the bar, pretty and attractive, ready to gossip with all comers. Nothing must interrupt that. You'd done your share, all that was necessary. And I—poor fool—I let you! I didn't insist—I gave in—"

"You wish to say—?" began Madame Maubert at last, breaking her silence.

"Yes! To say just that!" burst out Maubert. "Just that—you coward! When you might have—when you might have—made *this* out of the question for me." He shook his order for mobilisation. Again there was a noise from the kitchen, again the sound of many young voices, and one voice that ended in a cry, an irritated, angry, querulous howl.

"I see," said Madame Maubert slowly, "five instead of four— five would have made it safe for you—eh? I didn't think of that—at the time."

"Of your own self at the time—as always!" ground out Maubert, very angry. He was a very big man, of the bully type, with a red neck that swelled under his anger, or on the occasions when he had taken too much red wine—which meant that it swelled very often and made him a great brute, and his wife disliked him, and tried to put the zinc counter between them or anything else that gave shelter.

"You selfish coward!" he cried out again, and slammed his fist down, and then raised it again and shook it at her, "You could have saved me from this—this—being mobilised—! Five instead of four! Five instead of four! Then I would have been exempt, no matter what happened! You contemptible—"

He struck at his wife, but missed her. The doorway darkened and two soldiers entered, limping.

"My husband is mobilised," exclaimed Madame Maubert quickly. "His country needs him—he is rather elevated in consequence! Doubtless he will be of the auxiliaries, where there is less danger. Discomfort, perhaps, but less danger. Nevertheless he is regretful," she concluded scornfully. The simple soldiers, home on leave, laughed uproariously. They placed a few sous upon the counter and asked for wine, and drank to Maubert solicitously. Then they all drank together, to one another's good fortune, and to La Patrie.

Ellen Newbold La Motte

Maubert was at the Front. Near it, that is, but in the First Zone of the Armies and shut off from communication with the rear. He was shut off from communication with his wife and family, isolated in a little hut standing by the roadside, his sentry box. A little box of straw standing upright on the roadside, and with just enough room for him inside, also standing upright. No more. Whenever he heard the whir of a motor coming down the road, he opened his front door and stood squarely in the middle of the roadway, waving a red flag by day or a lantern by night, and expecting, both night and day, to be run down and killed by the onrushing motor. He flagged the ambulances and got cursed for it. He flagged the General's car and got cursed for it. Impossible pieces of paper were shoved out to him to read, filled with unintelligible hieroglyphics, which he could not read, which he made a vain pretence of reading and then concluded were all right. After which the car or the ambulance dashed on again, and he communed with himself within his hut, wondering whether the car was carrying a uniformed spy, or whether the ambulance was carrying a spy hidden under its brown wings, beneath the seat somewhere. It was all so perplexing and precarious, this business of sentry duty. The papers issued by the D.E.S. were so illegible. Sometimes they were blue, sometimes pink, and the remarks written on them were such that no one could understand or know what they were about. People had the right to circulate by this road or that—and when they were trying to circulate by a route not specified in the blue or pink paper, they always explained glibly that it was because they had missed the way, and made the wrong turning. It was all so perplexing. Whenever he stopped their cars, the General was always so furiously impatient, and the ambulance drivers were always so furiously impatient, and one asked you if you did not respect the Army of France, and the other if you did not respect the wounded of France, if you had no pity for them, and must delay them—altogether it was very perplexing. Maubert always had the impression that if he failed in his duties, if he let through a general who wore stripes and medals galore, yet who was a spy general, that he would be courtmartialed and shot. Or if he let through an ambulance full of wounded—apparently—yet with a spy concealed in the body—that he would be courtmartialed and shot. Always he had in his mind this fear of being courtmartialed and shot, and it made him very nervous, and he did not like to tell people that he could barely read and write. Very barely able to read and write, and totally unable to read the hieroglyphics written on the pink and blue papers issued down the road by Headquarters, at the D.E.S. He felt that some one ought to know these facts about himself, these extenuating circumstances, in case of trouble. Yet he hesitated to give himself away. Bad as it was, there were worse jobs than sentry duty.

A little way down the road there was an *estaminet*, where he slept when he could, where he spent his leisure hours, where he bought as much wine as he could pay for. But his sentry box always confronted him, which leaked when it rained, and the wind blew through it, and on certain days, when there was much travel by the road, he hardly spent a moment inside it but was always standing in the mud and wind of the highway, waving his flag, and stopping impatient, snorting motors. And always pretending that he could read the pink and blue papers, angrily thrust out for his inspection. Too great a responsibility for one who could barely read and write.

Came the time, eventually, for his leave. Five days permission. One day to get to Paris. One day from Paris to his province. One day in his province at home with his wife. One day back to Paris, one day to get back to his sentry box in the First Zone of the Armies. Not much time, all considered. He bought a bottle of wine at the *estaminet*, and got aboard the train for Paris. Somewhere along the route came a long stop, and he bought another bottle of wine—forty centimes. Another stop, and another bottle of wine. He thought much of his wife during these long hours of the journey—thoughts augmented and made glowing by three bottles of wine. She wasn't so bad, after all.

Ellen Newbold La Motte

The Gare Montparnasse was reached, and he got off, dizzily, to change trains. He knew, vaguely, that to get to his province in the interior, he must first somehow get to the Gare du Nord. There was a Metro entrance somewhere about the Gare Montparnasse and he tried to find it. The Metro would take him to the Gare du Nord. No good. Such crowds of people all about, and they called him Mon Vieux, and pulled him this way and that, laughing with him, offering him cigarettes and happy comments, received by a brain in which three bottles of wine were already fermenting. Thus it happened that he missed the Metro entrance, and instead of finding a metro to take him to the Gare du Nord, he missed the entrance, turned quite wrong, and walked up the middle of the rue de la Gaiete. And because of the three bottles of wine within him—entirely within his head—he walked light-heartedly up the rue de la Gaiete, with his helmet tossed backwards on his shaggy head, his heavy kit swinging in disordered fashion from his shoulders, his mouth open, shouting meaningless things to the passers-by, and his steps very short, jerky and unsteady. Thus it happened, that many people, seeing him in this condition, shuddered, and asked what France had come to, when she must place her faith in such men as that. Other people, however, laughed at him, and made way for him, or closed in on him and squeezed his arm, and whispered things into his ears. Back and forth he ricochetted along the narrow street, singing and swinging, mouth open, with strange, happy cries coming from it. Some laughed and said what a pity, and others laughed and said how perfectly natural and what could you expect.

Presently down the street came a big, double decked tramcar, and Maubert stood in front of the tramcar, refusing to give way. It should have presented a blue paper to him—or a pink paper—anyway, there he stood in front of it, asking for its permission to circulate, and as it had no permission, it stopped within an inch of running over him, while the conductor leaned forward shouting curses. Then it was that a firm but gentle hand inserted itself within Maubert's arm, while a firm but gentle voice asked Maubert to be a good boy and come with her. Maubert was very dazed, and also perplexed that he had not received a paper from the big, double-decked tramcar, which obviously had no right to circulate without such permission, sanctioned by himself. He was gently drawn off the tracks, by that unknown arm, while the big tramcar proceeded on its way without permission. It was all wrong, yet Maubert felt himself drawn to one side of the roadway, felt himself still propelled along by that gentle but firm arm, and looked to see who was leading him. He was quite satisfied by what he saw. The three bottles of wine made him very uncritical, but they also inflamed certain other faculties. To these other faculties his befogged mind gave quick response. To Hell with the tramcar, papers or no papers, pink or blue. Also, although not quite so emphatically, he relinquished all thoughts of arriving at the Gare du Nord, and of finding a train to take him home to his province, where his wife lived. The reasons that made him desire his wife, were quite satisfied with the gentle pressure on his arm. Thus it happened that big Maubert, shaggy and dirty and drunk, reeling down the rue de la Gaiete, very suddenly gave up all idea of finding his way to his province in the interior.

Never mind about those three days in Paris. Maubert was quite sober when he got on the train again at Montparnasse. He did not regret his larger vacation. He had had a very good permission, take it all in all.

III

At about the time that Maubert found himself mobilised and summoned into the reserves, a further mobilisation of subjects of the French Empire was taking place in certain little known, outlying dominions of the "Empire." I should have said Republic or even Democracy. The result, however, is all the same. In certain outlying portions of the mighty Empire or Republic or Democracy, as you will, further mobilisation of French subjects was taking place, although in these outlying dominions the forces were not mobilised but volunteered. That is to say, the headsman or chief of a certain village, lying somewhere between the Equator and ten degrees North latitude, was requested by those in authority to furnish so many volunteers. The word being thus passed round, volunteers presented themselves, voluntarily. Among them was Ouk. Ouk knew, having been so informed by the headsman of his village, that failure to respond to this opportunity meant a voluntary sojourn in the jungle. Ouk hated the jungle. All his life he had lived in terror of it, of the evil forces of the jungle, strangling and venomous, therefore he did not wish to take refuge amongst them, for he knew them well. Of the two alternatives, the risks of civilization seemed preferable. Civilization was an unknown quantity, whereas the jungle was familiar to himself and his ancestors, and the fear transmitted by his ancestors was firmly emplanted in his mind. Therefore he had no special desire to sojourn amongst the mighty forces of the forest, which he knew to be overwhelming. At that time, he did not know that the forces of civilization were equally sinister, equally overwhelming. All his belated brain knew, was that if he failed to answer the call of those in authority, he must take refuge in the forests. Which was sure death. It was sure death to wander defenceless, unarmed, in the twilight gloom of noon day, enveloped by dense overgrowth, avoiding venomous serpents and vile stinging insects by day, and crouching by night from man-eating tigers. It presented therefore, no pleasant alternative—no free wandering amidst beautiful, tropical trees and vines heavy with luscious fruits—

there would be no drinking from running streams in pleasant, sunlit clearings. Ouk knew the jungle, and as the alternative was civilization, he chose civilization which he did not yet know. Therefore he freely offered himself one evening, coming from his native village attired in a gay sarong, a peaked hat, and nothing more. He entered a camp, where he found himself in company with other volunteers, pressed into the service of civilization by the same pressure that had so appealed to himself. There were several hundred of them in this camp, all learning the ways of Europe, and learning with difficulty and pain. The most painful thing, perhaps, were the coarse leather shoes they were obliged to wear. Ouk's feet had been accustomed to being bare—clad, on extreme occasions, with pliant straw sandals. He garbed them now, according to instructions, in hard, coarse leather shoes, furnished by those in authority, which they told him would do much to protect his sensitive feet against the cold of a French winter. Ouk had no ideas as to the rigours of a French winter, but the heavy shoes were exceedingly painful. In exchange for his gay sarong, they gave him a thick, ill fitting suit of khaki flannel, in which he smothered, but this, they likewise explained to him, would do much to protect him from the inclemency of French weather. Thus wound up and bound up, and suffering mightily in the garb of European civilization, Ouk gave himself up to learn how to protect it. The alternative to this decision, being as we have said, an alternative that he could not bring himself to face.

Three months of training being accomplished, Ouk and his companions were by that time fitted to go forth for the protection of great ideals. They were the humble defenders of these ideals, and from time to time the newspapers spoke in glowing terms, of their sentimental, clamorous wish to defend them. Even in these remote, unknown regions, somewhere between the Equator and ten degrees North latitude, volunteers were pressing forward to uphold the high traditions of their masters. Ouk and his companions knew nothing of these sonorous, ringing phrases in the papers. They knew only of the alternative, the jungle. Time came and the day came

Ellen Newbold La Motte

when they were all ushered forth from their training camp, packed into a big junk, and released into the stormy tossings of the harbour, there to await the arrival of the French Mail, that was to convey them to Europe. The sun beat down hot upon them, in their unaccustomed shoes and khaki, the harbour waves tossed violently, and the French Mail was late. Eventually it arrived, however, and they all scrambled aboard, passing along a narrow gangplank from which four of them slipped and were drowned in the sea. But four out of five hundred was a small matter, quite insignificant.

When the French Mail arrived at Saigon, Ouk was able to replenish his supply of betel nut and sirra leaves, buying them from coolies in bobbing sampans, which sampans had been allowed to tie themselves to the other side of the steamer. At Singapore also he bought himself more betel nut and sirra leaves, but after leaving Singapore he was unable to replenish his stock, and consequently suffered. Every one with him, in that great company of volunteers, also suffered. It was an unexpected deprivation. The ship ploughed along, however, the officers taking small notice of Ouk and his kind—indeed, they only referred to Ouk by number, for no one of those in authority could possibly remember the outlandish names of these heathen. Nor did their names greatly matter.

Time passed, the long voyage was over, and Ouk landed at Marseilles. In course of time he found himself placed in a small town in one of the provinces, the very town from which Maubert had been released to go to the Front. Thus it happened that there were as many men in that town as had been taken away from it, only the colour and the race of the men had changed. The nationality of all of them, however, was the same—they were all subjects of the mighty French Empire or Democracy, and in France race prejudice is practically nil. Therefore Ouk, who worked in a munition factory, found himself regarded with curiosity and with interest, though not with prejudice. Thus it happened that Madame Maubert found herself gazing at Ouk one evening, from behind the safe security of her zinc covered bar. Curiosity and interest were in her soul, but no particular sense of racial superiority. Ouk and some companions, speaking together in heathen jargon, were seated comfortably at one of the little yellow tables of the cafe, learning to drink wine in place of the betel nut of which they had been deprived. All through the day they worked in one of the big factories, but in the evenings they were free, and able to mix with civilization and become acquainted with it. And they became acquainted with it in the bar of Madame Maubert, who served them with yellow wine, and who watched, from her safe place behind the zinc covered counter, the effect of yellow wine upon yellow bodies which presumably contained yellow souls—if any.

All this made its impression upon Ouk. All this enforced labour and civilization and unaccustomed wine. So it happened that one evening Ouk remained alone in the bar after his companions had gone, and he came close up to the zinc covered counter behind which was seated Madame Maubert, and he regarded her steadily. She too, regarded him steadily, and beheld in his slim, upright figure something which attracted her. And Ouk beheld in Madame Maubert something which attracted him. Seated upon her high stool on the other side of the counter, she towered above him, but he felt no awe of her, no sense of her superiority. True, she looked somewhat older than the girls in his village, but on the other hand, she had a pink and white skin, and Ouk had not yet come in contact with a pink and white skin. Nor had Madame Maubert ever seen, close to, the shining, beautiful skin of a young Oriental. After all, were they not both subjects of the same great nation, were they not both living and sacrificing themselves for the preservation of the same ideals? Madame Maubert had given up her man. Ouk had given up—heaven knows what—the jungle! Anyway, such being the effect of yellow wine upon Ouk, and such being the effect of Ouk on Madame Maubert, they both leaned their elbows upon opposite sides of the zinc counter that evening and looked at each other. For a whole year Madame Maubert's husband had been away from her, and for nearly a whole year Ouk had been away from the women of his kind, and suddenly they realised, gazing at each other from opposite sides of the zinc covered bar, that Civilization claimed them. Each had a duty to perform towards its furtherance and enhancement.

IV

Let us now go back to Maubert, standing for long months within his straw covered hut, or standing in the roadway in front of it, demanding passports. Every day, for many months past, he remembered his misspent permission and cursed the way he had passed it. Passed it in so futile a manner. Things might have been so different. His companions often chaffed him about it, chaffed him rudely. For he had never seen fit to tell them that he had not gone down to his home in the provinces, as they thought he had, but had been ensnared by some woman in Paris who had pulled him away from a passing tram on the rue de la Gaiete. One day the *vaguemestre* brought him a letter. He was very dizzy when he read it. Everything swam round. Rage and relief combated together in his limited brain. Rage and relief—rage and relief! He could take his letter to the authorities and demand his release—or—

For now he had five children, had Maubert. No one would question it. In his hand lay the letter of his wife. Five children. The fifth just born. That meant release from the service of his country. She said she was sorry. That she had done it for him. He would understand. But Maubert did not understand. He remembered his misspent permission, and the thought of it nauseated him. She, too. The thought of it nauseated him. Certainly he did not understand.

On the other hand, the authorities had on their books the date of his permission. He looked again at the letter of his wife. The dates coincided admirably. He had but to go to his superior officer and show him the letter of his wife, announcing the birth of their fifth child. Then he would be free. Free from the service of his country, the hated service, the examining of passports presented by a rushing General, by a rushing ambulance, by some rushing motor that was perhaps carrying a spy.

He so hated it all. But now, more than anything else, he hated his wife. He would accept his release and go home and kill her.

He wouldn't be free any more if he did that, however. He argued it out with himself. So he couldn't kill her. He must accept it. If he accepted his release from the service of his country, he must accept it on her terms. He spent a long day in the rain and the wind, thinking it out. But he thought it out at last. He would accept her terms, obtain his release, go home and see—and then decide.

He told his Colonel about it, and his Colonel chaffed him, and looked over some papers, and finally set in motion the mechanism by which he was finally set free from the service of his country. It took some weeks before this was accomplished, but it was finally done. And when he arrived in Paris, coming down from his post in the First Zone of the Armies, he was painfully sober. No more wine that day for him. No more wine, bought at the *estaminet* before he left, or bought during the long journey down to Paris. No more zig-zagging up the rue de la Gaiete. He found the Metro entrance at the exit of the Gare Montparnasse, took the train, and arrived, shortly afterwards, at the Gare du Nord, very sober. Very sober and angry.

And when he reached his home in the provinces, he was still sober and still angry. Nor did he know what he should do. He did not know whether he should kill his wife or not. If he did, he must go back to the Front. And he hated the Front. He hated his duties, sentry duty, in the First Zone of the Armies. He could not report to his Colonel again, and say, "Give me back my sentry box—let me serve my country—that fifth child is not mine!" He was in a tight place, surely. But at his home, his mood changed, his wife was very gentle. She said she had been wrong.

"Ouk is dead," she said. "All those poor little men who come from the Tropics die very soon in our cold, damp weather. They cannot stand it. The khaki flannels we give them do not warm them. There is not much wool in them. The cold penetrates into their bones. They catch cold and die, all of them, sooner or later. It is an extravagance, importing them."

Therefore he was mollified. "For your sake," said his wife. Maubert looked down at the fifth child lying in its cradle. The child that brought him release from the service of his country—release from sentry duty, from looking at hastily shoved out, unintelligible passports.

"For your sake," repeated his wife, slipping her arm through his arm. "Very well," said Maubert stiffly. All the same, he thought to himself, the child certainly looks like a Chinese.

MISUNDERSTANDING

I

They say out here, that one can never understand the native mind and its workings. So primitive are they, these quiet, gentle, brown-skinned men and women, crouching over their compound fires in the evening, lazily driving the lumbering buffaloes in the rice fields, living their facile life, here on the edge of the jungle. So primitive are they, these gentle, simple forest people.

In the towns—oh, but they are not made for the towns, they are so strangely out of place in the towns which the foreigner has contrived for himself on the borders of their brown, sluggish rivers, towns which he has created by pushing backward for a little the jungle, while he builds his pink and yellow bungalows beneath the palm trees, and spaces them between the banana trees, along straight tracks which he calls roads. Wide, red roads, which the natives have made under his direction, and deep, cool bungalows, which the natives have made under his direction. Altogether, they are his towns, the foreigners' towns, and he has constructed them so that they may remind him of his home, ten thousand miles across the world.

It is not necessary to try to fancy the natives in these foreign towns. They mean nothing to him, and are far distant from his tendencies and desires. His own villages are different—

thatched huts, erected on bamboo piles, roofed with palm leaves. They cluster close together along the winding brown rivers, on the edge of the jungle. Mounted very high on their stilts of bamboo, crowding each other very close together, compound touching compound for the sake of companionship and safety. Safety from the wild beasts of the forests, those that cry by night, and howl and prowl and kill; safety from the serpents, whose sting is death, shelter, protection, from all the dark, lurking dangers of the jungle—the evil, mighty forests, at whose edge, between it and the winding yellow rivers, they build themselves their homes. Yes, but life is very easy here, just the same. A little stirring of the rich earth in the clearings, and food springs forth. A little paddling up the stream or down, in a pirogue or a sampan, a net strung across the sluggish waters, and there is food again. A little wading in shallow, sunlit pools, a swift strike with a trident, and a fish is caught. And fruit hangs heavy from the trees. Life is very easy in these countries. And with the coming of the sudden sunset of the Tropics, the evening fires are lighted in the compounds and there is gathering together, with song and laughter, rest and ease. So as life is very facile in the jungle, love of money is unknown. Why money—what can it mean? Why toil for something which one has no use for, cannot spend? Just enough, perhaps, to bargain with the white man for some simple need—to buy a water buffalo, maybe, for ploughing in the rice fields. No more than that—it's not needed. And the very little coins, the very, very little coins, two dozen of them making up the white man's penny, just enough of these left over to stick upon the lips of Buddha, at the corners, with a little gum. Thus a prayer to Buddha, and the offering of a little coin, stuck with resin to the god's lips, as an offering. That is all. Life is very simple, living in one's skin.

I have said all this so that you might understand. Only, remember, no one understands, quite, the workings of the savage mind. And these of whom I write are gentle savages, and their way of life is simple, primitive and crude. Only, upon contact with the white man, some of this has been obliged to wear off a little. They have had to become adaptive, to assume a little polish, as it were. But at heart, after these many years of contact, they are still simple. They are mindless, gentle, squatting bare backed in the shade, chewing, spitting, betel nut. Chewing as the ox chews, thinking as the ox thinks. Gentle brown men and women, touching the edge of the most refined civilization of the western world.

The tale jerks here—why shouldn't it? The Lieutenant told me this bit of it himself—he lives in the foreigners' town, and keeps order there. There was a revolt last year. But that is too dignified a word, it assumes too much, it assumes something that there never was. For revolt signifies organisation, and there wasn't any. It signifies a general understanding, and there wasn't any. It signifies great numbers involved, and there were no great numbers. How could there have been any of these things, said the Lieutenant, among a scattered people, scattered through the jungle, on the edges of the warm, mighty forests, at the headwaters of the great winding rivers which penetrate inland for a thousand miles. No, it was in no sense a revolt, which is too strong a word. They had no organisation, they could not communicate with each other, had they wished. Distances were great, and they could not read or write. They had never been molested—never schooled. It was better so. Education is no good to a squatter in the shade. No, it was rather an uprising of a handful of them in the town of the white man, the town of red earth streets, with pink and yellow bungalows, cool and sheltered under spreading palms. The town where many foreigners lived, who walked about listlessly in their white linen clothes, ghastly pale, with dark rings beneath their eyes, who stifled in the heat and thought of Home, ten thousand miles away. It all happened suddenly, no one knows how or why. But one morning, just after the sun rose in his red, burning splendour, there crept into the town a few hundred men. They came in by this red street, with the statue of the Bishop at the top—the bronze statue of the Bishop who had lived and worked and died here years ago. They came by the red street leading past the bazaar, the model market, fashioned, with improvements, like the one at home. They came by the red street leading past the Botanical Garden, the gardens where at the close of scorching days the women of the white man, ghastly white, used to drive before sunset, to breathe a little after the stifling day. They came along the quais, where the white man's ships found harbour. Altogether, creeping in on many roads, coming in their fours and fives, they made about three hundred. And they were in revolt, if you please, against the representatives of the most refined civilization of the western world! Just three hundred, no more. Not a ripple of it, apparently, spread backwards to the jungle, to the millions inland, in the forests.

What happened? Oh, it was all over in an hour! The Lieutenant heard them coming—his orderly ran in with the word— and he was out in an instant with eight men. Eight soldiers armed with rifles. It was quite amusing. And opposed to them, that mob, in their peaked hats, in their loin cloths or their sarongs, bare to waist as usual. Poor fools! Fancy—not a gun among them! They thought they were invisible! The geomancer had told them that, and they believed him. Carried at their head a flag, some outlandish, homemade thing, with unknown characters upon it. Well, it was all over in a moment—those eight men armed with guns saw to that. Short work—thirty wounded, fourteen killed. The rest scattered, but before the day was out they had them—had them in two hours, for a fact. All disarmed, and the Lieutenant had their weapons. Come to see them at his bungalow, if we'd time? Interesting lot of trophies, most unique collection. Quite unequalled. Homemade spears, forged and hammered, stuck on bamboo poles. Homemade swords, good blades, too, for all their crudeness. Must have taken months to make them, fashioned slyly, on the quiet. Killing weapons, meant to kill. Swords like the Crusaders, only cased in bamboo scabbards. Funny lot—come to see them if we'd time. Nothing like it, a unique collection. And the flag—red cotton flag, all blood stained, with some device in corner, just barbaric. Poor fools! Flag pathetic? Pathetic? Heavens, no!

Well, they stamped it out very thoroughly, at four o'clock that afternoon. It finished at the race course, for there is always a

Ellen Newbold La Motte

race course where the white man rules. Word went round, as it always goes round in times like this, and just before sunset the whole native population was out to see the white man's method. No one hindered them or feared them, for apparently they had no hand in this uprising, and moreover, were unarmed. They were full of curiosity to see what they should see. Silently they trooped out in hundreds through the shady, palm bordered, red streets of the town, padding barefoot past the sheltered bungalows, past the bronze statue of the Bishop, out to the edge of the town. All the Tropics was there, moving silently, flowing gently, in their hundreds, to the race course. Dark skins, yellow skins, eyes straight, eyes slanting, black hair cut short, or worn in pigtails, or in top knots, or in chignons; bare bodies, bare legs, or legs clothed in brilliant sarongs or in flapping pyjamas—all the costumes of all the countries bordering the Seven Seas streamed outward from the town, very silent. And as the sun blazed low to his setting; all the Tropics waited to see what the white man would do.

They did it very cleverly, the white men. For they called upon the native troops to do it for them, to see if they were loyal. There were thirty-four prisoners all told, and they walked along with hands bound behind them, looking very stupid. Even as they walked along, at that moment the wife of the Lieutenant was showing their crude spears to friends—she gave tea to her friends in the pink bungalow, and exhibited the captured weapons, but the Lieutenant was not there—he was at the race course, supervising.

They led them forward in groups of six, and they were faced by six native soldiers armed with rifles. And just behind the six native soldiers stood six soldiers of the white troops, also with rifles. And when the word was given to fire, if the native troops had not fired upon their brothers, the white troops would have fired upon both. It was cleverly managed, and very well arranged. But there was no hitch. Six times the native troops fired upon batches of naked, kneeling men, and six times the white soldiers stood behind them with raised rifles, in case of hesitation. Only the crack of the rifles broke the stillness. The dense crowd of natives gathered close, standing by in silence. Giving no sign, they watched the retribution of the white man. The sun beat down upon them, in their wide hats, their semi-nakedness, attired in their sombre or brilliant cotton skirts. When it was over, they dispersed as quietly as they had gathered. The silent crowds walked back from the race course, the pleasure ground of the dominant race, and drifted along the red streets of the town, back again to the holes and burrows from which they had come.

II

A year later, nearly. The Lieutenant who had quelled the uprising, with a handful of men armed with rifles of the latest device, as against three hundred natives armed with spears, had been decorated and was very proud. He also continued to exhibit his unique collection of arms to all comers, when the mail boats came in. Nor did he see their pathos. And in the jungles of the interior, where most of them lived, the natives never knew of the existence of the little red flag, and would not have understood if they had been told. Why? The white men were kind and considerate. Easy and indulgent masters who in no wise interfered with life as lived in the jungle. But with the native troops who had fired upon their brothers it was different.

Thus it happened that the small coastwise steamer, going her usual cruise among the islands and along the coast of one of the Seven Seas, carried unusual freight. Being a very little boat, with a light cargo, she was sometimes severely buffeted by the northeast monsoon, which was blowing at that time of the year. On these days, when the monsoon was strongest, the few passengers she carried were not comfortable. On other days, when she found calm weather among the islands, it was very pleasant. She dropped anchor from time to time in little bays bordered with cocoanut tree, and from the bays emerged sampans with vivid painted eyes on their prows, seeking out the steamer and the bales of rice she carried, or the mails. The mails, consisting of half a dozen letters for each port, were tied up in big canvas sacks, sealed with big government seals, and the white men who lived on these remote, desert islands, would come themselves to fetch them. They paddled themselves to the steamer in pirogues or in sampans, white faced, anaemic, apathetic, devoid of vitality. The great, overwhelming heat of the Tropics, the isolation of life, in unknown islands in the southern seas, makes one like that. Yet they were "making money" on their island plantations of rubber or cocoanut, or expecting to make it. It takes seven years of isolation in the tropic seas, after one has started a plantation—and even then, many things may happen—

So the little steamer stopped here and there, at little, unknown bays, at places not mentioned in the guide books, and from the beautiful, desolate islands came out sampans and junks, with the lonely figure of a white man sitting despondent among the naked rowers, eager to get his letters from home. It was his only eagerness, but very dull and listless at that. At night, the islands loomed large and mysterious in the darkness, while now and then a single ray of light from some light house, gleaming from some lost, mysterious island of the southern seas, beamed with a curious constancy. There were dangerous rocks, sunken reefs. And always the soft wind blew, the soft, enervating wind of the Tropics.

On the fore part of the little steamer, that wound its way with infinite care, slowly, among the sunken rocks, the shoals and sandbars, sat a company of fifty men. Natives, such as you might see back there in the jungle, or harnessed to the needs of civilization, bearing the white man in rickshaws along the red streets of the little town. These, however, were native troops— the rickshaw runner used in another way. They were handcuffed together, sitting in pairs on the main deck. In the soft, moist wind, they eat rice together, with their free hands, out of the same bowl. Very dirty little prisoners, clad in khaki, disarmed, chained together in pairs. A canvas was stretched over that part of the deck, which sheltered them from the glaring sun, and prevented the odour of them from rising to the bridge, a little way above, where stood the Captain in yellow crepe pyjamas. For they were dirty, handcuffed together like that, unexercised, unwashed. They would be put ashore in three days, however, to work on the roads, government roads. Notoriously good roads, the colony has too. Their offense? Grave enough. With the European world at war, this colony, like those of all the other nations, had called upon its native troops. The native troops had been loyal, had responded, had volunteered to go when told they must. Proof of that? Forty thousand of them at the moment helping in this devastating war. It was a good record—it spoke well—

Only this handful had refused. Refused absolutely, flagrantly defiant. Just this little group, out of all the thousands. So they were being sent off somewhere, handcuffed, to make roads. Prisoners for three years to make roads, useless roads that led nowhere. Good roads, excellent, for traffic that never was. Some said they were the soldiers who had been forced to kill their brothers a while back—after that paltry revolution. One didn't know. They are stupid, these natives. Chewing betel nut all day, their mouths a red, bloody gash across their faces.

The ship stopped finally in some bay. Then a big, unwieldy junk put out from shore, and tacked back and forth, for two hours, against a strong head wind, coming to rest finally against the steamer's side. Two big iron rods were put out, with a padlock at each end, and places for twenty-five feet to be locked in. Then came European guards, with rifles, and revolvers in big leather cases hanging at their sides. The prisoners were very docile, but it was well to take precautions. When all was ready, the prisoners filed out slowly and with difficulty, because of their chains, and descended the gangway ladder to the uncouth junk, with its painted, staring eyes. After that, the junk slowly detached itself from the ship, unrolled its ragged matting sails, and made towards the mainland with the docile cargo.

The third passenger leaned over the rail. A sweet breeze blew in from the island, a scented breeze, laden with the heavy scents of the Tropics. For three years, he said, they would labour at the futile roads, the roads that led nowhere. Really, commented the third passenger, it was impossible to understand the Oriental mind. They had chosen this—this isolation, this cutting off from home and friends, rather then go to Europe to serve the race that had treated them so well. Afraid? Oh, no—too ignorant to be afraid. Brave enough when it came to that—just obstinate. Just refused to serve, to do as they were told. Refused to serve, to fight for the race that had treated them so well, by and large, take it all in all. That had

built them towns and harbours, brought in ships and trade—
had done everything, according to best western standards. It
was incomprehensible—truly it was difficult to fathom the
Oriental mind! The revolt a year ago? Oh, nothing!

The big junk with the staring eyes carried them off, the supine,
listless prisoners, handcuffed together, foot-locked to an iron
bar. They must build roads for three years. Somewhere at the
back of those slow minds was a memory of the race course, of
the brothers they had slain. Perhaps. Who knows. But the
Occidental mind does not understand the Oriental mind, and
it was good to be rid of them, dirty little creatures, who
smelled so bad under the awning of the main deck.

The anchor chain wound in, grating link on link. The soft,
sweet wind blew outward from the cocoanut trees, from the
scented earth of the island. The third passenger watched the
junk disappear in the shadows of the warm night, then he went
below to get another drink.

PRISONERS

Mercier was writing his report for the day. He sat at a rattan table, covered with a disorderly array of papers, ledgers and note books of various sorts, and from time to time made calculations on the back of an old envelope. He finally finished his work, and pushing back his chair, lighted a cigarette. Unconsciously, he measured time by cigarettes. One cigarette, and he would begin work. One cigarette and he would start on the first paragraph. One cigarette, to rest after the first paragraph before beginning the second, and so on. It was early in the morning, but not early for a morning in the Tropics. Already the sun was creeping over the edge of the deep, palm-shaded verandah, making its way slowly across the wooden floor, till it would reach him, at his table, in a very short time. And as it slowly crept along, a brilliant line of light, so the heat increased, the moist, stagnant heat, from which there was no escape. Outside some one was pulling the punkah rope, and the great leaves of linen, attached to heavy teak poles, swayed back and forth over his head, stirring slightly the dense, humid atmosphere.

Mercier was a young man, not over thirty. He had come out to the East three years ago, to a minor official post in the Penal Settlement, glad of a soft position, of easy work, of an opportunity to see life in the Tropics. At a port on the mainland, he transshipped from the liner to a little steamer, which two days later dropped anchor in the blue bay of his future home. At that time, he was conscious of being intensely pleased at the picture spread before him. Long ago, in boyhood, he had cherished romantic dreams of the Tropics, of islands in southern seas, of unknown, mysterious life set in gorgeous, remote setting. It had all appealed to his fancy, and then suddenly, after many long years, sordid, difficult years, the opportunity had come for the realisation of his dreams. He had obtained a post as minor official in one of the colonies of his country—overseas in the Far East—and he gladly gave up his dull, routine life at home, and came out to the adventures that awaited him. The island, as he saw it for the first time, was beautiful. Steep hills, rocky and mountainous, rose precipitately out of the blue waters, and the rising sun glinted upon the topmost peaks of the hills and threw their deep shadows down upon the bay, and upon the group of yellow stucco bungalows that clustered together upon the edge of the water, upon the narrow strip of land lying between the sea and the sheer sides of the backing mountains. The bay was a crescent, almost closed, and a coral reef ran in an encircling sweep from the headland beyond, and the translucent, sparkling waters of the harbour seemed beautiful beyond belief. His heart beat wildly when for the first time he beheld his new home—it exceeded in beauty anything that he had ever dreamed of. What mattered it whether or no it was a Penal Settlement for one of the great, outlying colonies of his mother country, two days' sail from the nearest port on the mainland, the port itself ten thousand miles from home. It was beautiful to look upon—glorious to look upon, and it was glorious to think that the next few years of his life would be spent amidst such surroundings. The captain of the coasting steamer told him it would be lonely—he laughed at the idea. How could one be lonely amidst such beauty as that! His thirsty soul craved beauty, and here it was before him, marvellous, complete, the island a gem sparkling in the sunlight, veiled in the shadow of an early morning. Lying somewhere, all this beauty, one degree north or south of the Equator!

No, assuredly, he would not be lonely! Were there not many families on the island, the officials and their families, a good ten or fifteen of them? Besides, there was his work. He knew nothing of his work, of his duties. But in connection with the

Ellen Newbold La Motte

prisoners, of course—and there were fifteen hundred prisoners, they told him, concentrated on those few square miles of island, off somewhere in the Southern Seas, a few miles north or south of the Equator. He was anxious to see the prisoners, the unruly ones of the colony. Strange types they would appear to his conventional, sophisticated eyes. He saw them in imagination—yellow skins, brown skins, black skins, picturesque, daring, desperate perhaps. The anchor splashed overboard into the shallow water, and the small steamer drifted on the end of the chain, waiting for a boat to come out from shore. With the cessation of the steamer's movement, he felt the heat radiate round him, in an overpowering wave, making him feel rather sick and giddy. Yet it was only six o'clock in the morning. Before the boat arrived from shore, the sun had passed over the highest peak of the mountains and was glaring down with full power upon the cluster of hidden bungalows, the edges and ends of which bungalows protruded a little from the shelter of vines and palm trees. White clad men came down to the beach, and a woman or two appeared on the verandahs, and then disappeared back into the verandahs, while the men came down to the water's edge alone. The rowboat was pulled ashore by strong rowers, dark skinned, brawny men, and as the boat neared the beach, other dark skinned brawny men took a carrying chair and splashed out to meet the boat, inviting him by gestures to step into the chair and be carried ashore. He forgot the heat in the novelty of this new sensation—being carried ashore in a chair, with the clear, transparent water beneath him, and wavy sands, shell studded, over which the bearers walked slowly, with precision. And then came his first hours on shore. How calmly they had welcomed him, those white faced, pale men, with the deep circles beneath their eyes. They looked at him with envy, it seems, as a being newly come from contact with civilization, and they looked upon him with pity, as a being who had deliberately chosen to shut himself off from civilization, for a period of many years. He was taking the place of one who was going home—and the man was in a desperate hurry to get away. He looked ill, withal he was so fat, for he was very fat and flabby, extraordinarily white, with circles beneath his puffy eyes blacker and more marked than those on the other faces. The departing official shook hands hurriedly with Mercier, and kissed his old companions good-bye hurriedly upon both cheeks, and then hastened into the chair, to get to the rowboat, to get to the steamer as soon as possible. The other officials on the beach commented volubly on his good fortune—ah, but he had the chance! What chance! What luck! What fortune! They themselves had no luck, they must remain here how long, ah, who knew how long! They all stood there upon the beach watching the departing one until he reached the steamer, drifting idly at the length of her anchor chain.

Then they remembered Mercier again, and surrounded him, not eagerly, listlessly, and asked him to the office of the Administrator, to have a cup of champagne. A cup of champagne, at a little after six in the morning. As they walked slowly up the beach, Mercier spoke of the beauty of the place, the extraordinary beauty of the island. They seemed not to heed him. They smiled, and reminded him that he was a newcomer, and that such was the feeling of all newcomers and that it would soon pass. And in a body, ten of them, they conducted Mercier to the bureau of the Administrator, a tired, middle aged men, who shook hands without cordiality, and ordered a boy to bring a tray with a bottle and glasses and mouldy biscuits, and they all sat together and drank without merriment. It was dark in the Administrator's office, for the surrounding verandah was very wide and deep, and tall bamboos grew close against the edges of the railing, and a little way behind the bamboos grew banana trees and travellers' palms, all reaching high into the air and making a thick defence against the sunlight. The stone floor had been freshly sprinkled with water, and the ceiling was high, made of dark teak wood, and it was very dark inside, and damp and rather cool. There was a punkah hanging from the ceiling, but it stood at rest. Its movement had come to make the Administrator nervous. He was very nervous and restless, turning his head from side to side in quick, sharp jerks, first over one shoulder and then the other, and now and then suddenly bending down to glance under the table. Later on,

Ellen Newbold La Motte

some one explained to Mercier that the Administrator had a profound fear of insects, the fierce, crawling, stinging things that lived outside under the bamboos, and that crept in sometimes across the stone paved floor, and bit. Only last week, one of the paroled convicts, working in the settlement, had been bitten by some venomous evil thing, and had died a few hours later. Such accidents were common—one must always be on guard. Most people became used to being on guard, but with the Administrator, the thing had become a nightmare. He had been out too long—his nerves were tortured. It was the heat, of course—the stifling, enervating heat. Few could stand it for very long, and the authorities back home must have forgotten to relieve the old man—he was such a good executive, perhaps they had forgotten on purpose. The sub-officials were changed from time to time, but the old man seemed to have been forgotten. He could not stand it much longer—that was obvious.

Mercier went thoughtfully to the bungalow assigned to him, installed his few meagre possessions, and entered without zest upon his work. Somehow, the keenness had been taken out of him by that hour's conversation in the darkened bureau of the Chief. The weeks passed slowly, but Mercier never regained his enthusiasm. The physical atmosphere took all initiative away. His comrades were listless beings, always tired, dragging slowly to their daily rounds, and finishing their work early in the morning before the heat became intolerable. Then for hours they rested—retired to their bungalows or that of a comrade, and rested, to escape the intense heat which never varied, winter or summer, although it was a farce to speak of the seasons as winter or summer, except in memory of home. Mercier soon fell in with their ways. He drank a great deal, beginning very early in the morning, and measured time by cigarettes, postponing his duties, such that claimed him, till he had just finished another cigarette. They were cheap and bad, but there was a solace in them, and they whiled away the time. The only joviality about the place came in the evenings, after many cigarettes, which made him nervous, and after very many little glasses of brandy, which unfitted him for work but which were necessary to stimulate him for what work he had to do.

Near the group of bungalows belonging to the officials and to the prison guards, stood the prison building itself, a large, rambling, one storeyed structure, with many windows fitted with iron bars. Here the newcomers were kept, about eight hundred of them, and nearby, in an adjacent compound, were quarters for about seven hundred prisoners out on parole, by reason of good conduct. The confined prisoners did not work, being merely confined, but those out on parole, on good conduct, and whose terms would soon come to an end, were trusted to work about the island in various capacities. They made the roads—such few as there were. The island was so small that many roads were not required, and since there was no traffic, but little labour was required to keep the roads in repair. They also worked in the rice fields, but, again, there were not many rice fields. It was easier to bring rice from the mainland. There was a herd of water buffaloes, used for ploughing during the season, and the buffaloes needed some attention, but not much. So the paroled convicts were employed in other ways about the island, in cooking for the prisoners, in cleaning the various buildings, and as servants in the households of the officials. Only the most trusted, however, were given such posts as that. Yet it was necessary to trust many of them, and each official had a large retinue of servants, for there was little settlement work to be done, and something must be done with the men on parole, since the prison itself was too small to hold fifteen hundred men under lock and key at the same time. Moreover, these trusted ones were rather necessary. In the Tropics, work is always done in a small, half-hearted way, by reason of the heat which so soon exhausts the vitality, consequently many people are required to perform the smallest task.

Mercier, therefore, was obliged to accept the life as he found it, and he found it different from the romantic conception which he had formed at home. And he became very listless and demoralised, and the lack of interests of all sorts bored him intolerably. He was not one to find solace in an intellectual life. The bi-monthly call of the supply ship with its stocks of provisions, the unloading of which he must oversee, was the sole outside interest he had to look forward to. Old newspapers and magazines came with the supply ship, and these were eagerly read, and soon abandoned, and nothing was left but cigarettes and brandy to sustain him between whiles.

On a certain morning, when he had been at the settlement for over a year, he finished his daily report and strolled over to lay it upon the desk in the office of the Administrator. The supply ship was due in that day, and he wandered down to the beach to look for her. There she was, just dropping anchor. His heart beat a little faster, and he hastened his steps. It was cattle day. Bullocks from the mainland, several hundred miles away, which came once a month for food. He took his boat and rowed, out to the ship, and then directed the work of removing the bullocks.

It was nasty work. The coolies did it badly. The hatch was opened, and by means of a block and pulley, each bullock was dragged upward by a rope attached to its horns. Kicking and struggling, they were swung upwards over the side of the ship and lowered into the lighter below. Sometimes they were swung out too far and landed straddle on the side of the lighter, straddling the rail, kicking and roaring. And sometimes, when the loosely moored lighter drifted away a little from the ship's side, an animal would be lowered between the ship's side and the lighter, and squeezed between the two—so crushed that when it was finally hauled up and lowered safely into the boat, it collapsed in a heap, with blood flowing from its mouth. The coolies did it all very badly—they had no system, and as Mercier could not speak to them in their language, he could not direct them properly. Besides, he was no organiser himself, and probably could not have directed them properly had he been able to speak to them. All he could do, therefore, was to look on, and let them do it in their own way. Sometimes as an animal was being raised, its horns would break, and it would be lowered with a bleeding head, while the coolies stood by and grinned, and considered it a joke. Mercier was still sensitive on some points, and while long ago he had ceased to find any beauty in the island, he was nevertheless disgusted with needless suffering, with stupid, ugly acts.

There were only twenty cattle to be unloaded on this day, but it took two hours to transfer them to the lighter, and at the end of that time the tide had fallen so that they must wait for another six or eight hours, in the broiling sun, until the water was high enough for the lighter to approach the landing stage, where another block and pulley was rigged. Which meant that later in the day—possibly in the hottest part—Mercier would be obliged to come down again to oversee the work, and to see that it was finished. For the cattle must be ashore by evening— meat was needed for the settlement, and some must be killed for food that night. Mercier was thoroughly disgusted with his work, with his whole wasted life. Ah, it was a dog's life! Yet how eagerly he had tried to obtain this post—how eagerly he had begged for the chance, pleaded for it, besought the few influential people he knew to obtain it for him.

On the way back to his bungalow, he passed along the palm grown road, on each side of which were the red and white bungalows, residences of the dozen officials of the island. They were screened by hedges of high growing bushes, bearing brilliant, exotic flowers which gave out a heavy, sweet perfume, and the perfume hung in clouds, invisible yet tangible, pervading the soft, warm air. How he had dreamed of such perfumes—long ago. Yet how sickening in reality. And how dull they were, the interiors of these sheltered bungalows, how dull and stupid the monotonous life that went on inside them—dejected, weary, useless little rounds of household activity, that went along languorously each day, and led nowhere. It all led nowhere. Within each house was the wearied, stupid wife of some petty official, and sometimes there were stupid, pallid children as well, tended by convicts on parole. Nowhere could he turn to find intellectual refreshment. The community offered nothing—there was no society—just the dull daily greetings, the dull, commonplace comments on island doings or not doings, for all lay under the

Ellen Newbold La Motte

spell of isolation, under the pall of the great, oppressive, overwhelming heat. How deadly it all was, the monotonous life, the isolation, the lack of interests and occupation. As he passed along, a frowzy woman in a Mother Hubbard greeted him from a verandah and asked him to enter. Years ago she had come out fresh and blooming, and now she was prematurely aged, fat and stupid—more stupid, perhaps, than the rest. Yet somehow, because there was nothing else to do, Mercier pushed open the flimsy bamboo gate, walked up the gravelled path, and flung himself dejectedly upon a chaise longue which was at hand. And the woman talked to him, asked him how many cattle had come over that morning, whether they were yet unloaded, when they would be finally landed and led to the slaughter pens a little way inland. It was all so gross, so banal, yet it was all there was of incident in the day, and most clays were still more barren, with not even these paltry events to discuss. And he felt that he was sinking to the level of these people, he who had dreamed of high romance, of the mystery of the Far Eastern Tropics! And this was what it meant—what it had come to! A fat woman in a Mother Hubbard asking him how many bullocks had come in that day, and when they would be ready to kill and eat!

She clapped together her small, fat hands, and a servant entered, and she ordered grenadine and soda and liqueurs, and pushed towards him a box of cheap cigarettes. Where was her charm? Why had he married her, her husband—who was at the moment in the Administrator's bureau, compiling useless statistics concerning the petty revenues of the prison colony? But he was just like her, in his way. All the men were run to seed, and all their women too. And these were the only women on the island, these worn, pale, bloated wives who led an idle life in the blazing heat. Seven such women, all told. He relapsed into silence, and she likewise fell silent, there being nothing more to get nor give. They were all gone, intellectually. They had no ideas, nothing to exchange. So he smoked on, lazily, in silence, feeling the slight stir in his blood caused by the Quinquina. He filled his glass again, and looked forward to the next wave of relaxation. Overhead, the punkah swung slowly, stirring the scented air. These were the scents he had dreamed of, the rich, heavy perfumes of the Tropics. Only it was all so dull!

The door opened and a little girl entered the verandah, a child of perhaps fourteen. A doomed child. He looked at her languidly, and continued to look at her, thinking vague thoughts. She was beautiful. Her cotton frock, belted in by some strange arrangement of seashells woven into a girdle, pressed tightly over her young form, revealing clearly the outline of a childish figure soon ready to bloom into full maturity under these hot rays of vertical sunshine. She would develop soon, even as the native women developed into maturity very early. His tired glance rested upon her face. That, too, bore promise of great beauty. The features were fine and regular, singularly well formed, and the eyes those of a gentle cow, unspeculative, unintelligent. She was very white, with the deathlike whiteness of the Tropics, and under the childish eyes were deep, black rings, coming early. He noticed her hands—slender, long, with beautiful fingernails—such hands in Paris! And again his roving glance fell lower, and rested upon her bare legs, well formed, well developed, the legs of a young woman. He stirred lightly in his chair. The feet matched the hands—slender, long feet, with long, slender toes. She was wearing native sandals, clumsy wooden sandals, with knobs between the first two toes. Only the knobs were of silver, instead of the usual buttons of bone, or wood. Some one had brought them to her from the mainland, evidently. Well, here she was, a doomed creature, uneducated, growing older, growing into womanhood, with no outlook ahead. Her only companions her dull, stupid mother, and the worn-out wives of the officials—all years older than herself. Or perhaps she depended for companionship upon the children—there were a dozen such, about the place, between the ages of two and six. And she stood between these two groups, just blooming into womanhood, with her beautiful young body, and her atrophied young brain. Her eyes fell shyly under his penetrating, speculative glances, and a wave of colour rose into her white cheeks. She felt, then, hey? Felt what?

Mercier leaned forward, with something curious pulsing in his breast. The sort of feeling that he had long since forgotten, for there was nothing for such feelings to feed upon, here in his prison. Yet the sensation, vague as it was, seemed to have been recognised, shared for an instant by the young creature beside him. It was rather uncanny. He had heard that idiots or half-witted people were like that. She rose uneasily, placing upon her long, sprawling curls an old sun hat, very dirty, the brim misshapen by frequent wettings of pipe-clay. A servant appeared from behind the far corner of the verandah, an old man, dark skinned, emaciated, clad in a faded red sarong. He was her personal servant, told off to attend her. Something must be done for the men on parole, some occupation given them to test their fitness before returning them again to society. As she passed from the verandah, followed by the old black man in his red sarong, Mercier felt a strange thrill. Where were they going, those two?

He turned to the inattentive, vacuous mother. "Your daughter," he began, "is fast growing up. Soon she will be marrying."

The woman shrugged her shoulders.

"With whom?" she answered. "Who will take her? What dowry can we give her? We cannot even send her to Singapore to be educated. Who will take her—ignorant, uneducated—without a *dot*? Besides," she continued eagerly, warmed into a burst of confidence, "you have heard—you have seen—the trouble lies here," and she tapped her forehead significantly.

And with a sigh she concluded, "We are all prisoners here, every one of us—like the rest."

Mercier rose from the chaise longue, still thinking deeply, still stirred by the vague emotion that had called forth an answer from the immature, half-witted child. He had a report to make to the Bureau, and he must be getting on. Later, when the tide turned, and the lighter could come against the jetty, he must attend to the cattle.

He did not linger in the office of the Administrator, but sent in his report by a waiting boy, and then strolled inland by the road that led past the prison, into the interior of the island. On his way he passed the graveyard. It was a melancholy graveyard, containing a few slanting shafts erected to the memory of guards and of one or two officers who had been killed from time to time by prisoners who had run amok. Such uprisings occurred now and then, but seldom. He entered the cemetery, and looked about languidly, reading the names on the stones. Killed, killed, killed. Then he came upon a few who had died naturally. Or was it natural to have died, at the age of thirty, out here on the edge of the world? Yet it was most natural, after all. He himself was nearly ready for the grave, ready because of pure boredom, through pure inertia, quite ready to succumb to the devitalising effect of this life. This hideous life on a desert island. This hideous mockery of life, lived while he was still so young and so vital, and which was reducing him, not slowly but with great pacing strides, to an inertia to which he must soon succumb. Why didn't the prisoners revolt now, he wondered? He would gladly accept such a way out—gladly offer himself to their knives, or their clubs, or whatever it was they had. Anything that would put an end to him, and land him under a stone in this forsaken spot. Surely he was no more alive than the dead under those stones. No more dead than the dead.

He passed out of the gate, swinging on a loose hinge, and in deep meditation walked along the palm bordered road back of the settlement. Soon the last bungalow was left behind, even though he walked slowly. Then succeeded the paddy fields, poorly tilled and badly irrigated. There were enough men on the island to have done it properly—only what was the use? Who cared—whether they raised their own rice or brought it from the mainland twice a month? It was not a matter to bother about. Water buffaloes, grazing by the roadside, raised their heavy heads and stared at him with unspeakable insolence. They were for ploughing the rice fields, but who

Ellen Newbold La Motte

had the heart to oversee the work? Better leave the men squatting in content by the roadside, under the straggly banana trees, than urge them to work. It meant more effort on the part of the officials and effort was so useless. All so futile and so hopeless. He nodded in recognition of the salutes given him by groups of paroled prisoners, chewing betel nut under the trees. Let them be.

A bend in the road brought him to a halt. Just beyond, lying at full length upon the parched grass, was the little girl he had seen that morning. She lay on her back, with bare legs extended, asleep. Nearby, squatting on his heels and lost in a meditative pipe, sat the Kling, her body servant. The man rose to his feet respectfully as Mercier passed, watching his mistress and watching Mercier with a sombre eye. Mercier passed on slowly, with a long glance at the child. She was not a child, really. Her cotton dress clung round her closely, and he gazed fascinated, at the young figure, realising that it was mature. Mature enough. A thought suddenly rose to his mind, submerging everything else. He walked on hurriedly, and at a turn of the road, looked back. The Kling was sitting down again impassively, refilling his pipe.

From that time on, Mercier's days were days of torment, and the nights as well. He struggled violently against this new feeling, this hideous obsession, and plunged into his work violently, to escape it. But his work, meagre and insufficient at best, was merely finished the sooner because of his energy, which left him with more time on his hands. That was all. Time in which to think and to struggle. No, certainly, he did not wish to marry. That thought was put aside immediately. Marry a stupid little child like that, with a brain as fat as her body! But not as beautiful as her body. Besides, she was too young to marry, even in the Tropics, where all things mate young. But there she was, forever coming across his path at every turn. In his long walks back into the interior, behind the settlement, he came upon her daily, with her attendant Kling. The Kling always squatting on his heels, smoking, or else rolling himself a bit of areca nut into a sirrah-leaf, and dabbing on a bit of pink lime from his worn, silver box. Mercier tried to talk to the child, to disillusion himself by conversations which showed the paucity of ideas, her retarded mentality. But he always ended by looking at the beautiful, slim hands, at the beautiful, slim feet, at the cotton gown slightly pressed outward by the maturing form within.

He was angry with himself, furious at the obsession that possessed him. Once he entered the gravelled path of the child's home, and seriously discussed with her mother the danger of letting her roam at large over the island, accompanied only by the old Kling. He explained vigorously that it was not safe. There were hundreds of paroled prisoners at large, engaged in the ricefields, on the plantations, mending the roads—there was not a native woman on the place. He explained and expostulated volubly, surprised at his own eloquence. The mother took it calmly. The Kling, she replied, was trustworthy. He was an old man, very trustworthy and very strong. No harm could come to her daughter under his protection. And the long rambles abroad were good for the child. Was she not accustomed to convicts, as servants? She had a houseful of them, and many years' experience. What did he know of them, a comparative newcomer? For example, she had three pirates, Malays from the coast of Siam. They were quiet enough now. And one Cambodian, a murderer, true enough, but gentle enough now. Three house-boys and a cook. As for the old Kling, he was a marvel—he had been a thief in his day, but now—well now, he was body-servant for her daughter and a more faithful soul it would be hard to find. For seven years she had lived upon the island, surrounded by these men. She knew them well enough. True, there was the graveyard back of the prison compound, eloquent, mute testimony of certain lapses from trustworthiness, but she was not afraid. She had no imagination, and Mercier, failing to make her sense danger, gave it up. It had been a great effort. He had been pleading for protection against himself.

Mercier awoke one morning very early. It was early, but still dark, for never, in these baleful Tropics, did the dawn precede

Ellen Newbold La Motte

the sunrise, and there was no slow, gradual greying and rosying creeping of daylight, preceding the dawn. It was early and dark, with a damp coolness in the air, and he reached down from his cot for his slippers, and first clapped them together before placing them upon his slim feet. Then he arose, stepped out upon his verandah, and thought awhile. Darkness everywhere, and the noise of the surf beating within the enclosed crescent of the harbour. Over all, a great heat, tinged with a damp coolness, a coolness which was sinister. And standing upon his verandah, came rushing over him the agony of his wasted life. His prisoner life upon this lonely island in the Southern Seas. Exchanged, this wasted life, for his romantic dreams, and a salary of a few hundred francs a year. That day he would write and ask for his release—send in his resignation —although it would be weeks or months before he could be relieved. As he stood there in agony, the dawn broke before him suddenly, as Tropic dawns do break, all of a sudden, with a rush. Before him rose the high peaks of the binding mountains, high, impassable, black peaks, towering like a wall of rock. It was the wall of the world, and he could not scale it. Before him stretched the curve of the southern sea, in a crescent, but for all its fluidity, as impassable as the backing wall of rock. Between the two he was hemmed in, on a narrow strip of land, enclosed between the mountain wall and the curving reach of sea. He and all his futile interests lay within that narrow strip of land, between the mountain wall and the sea—and the strip was very narrow and small.

He went forth from his bungalow, pulling upon his feet clumsy native sandals of wood, with a button between the toes. For underfoot lay the things he dreaded, the heat things, the things bred by this warm climate enclosed between the high wall of the mountains and the infitting curve of the sea. He tramped awkwardly along in his loose fitting sandals, fast at the toe, clapping up and down at the heel. The one street of the town through which he passed was bordered by the houses of the officials, all sleeping. They were accustomed to sleeping. Only he, Mercier, could not sleep. He was not yet accustomed to being a prisoner. Perhaps—in time—

He clapped along gently, though to him it seemed very noisily, past the bungalows of the officials, past the big prison, also sleeping. Past the Administration buildings, past the weed-grown, unused tennis courts, out upon the red road leading to the mountains. Turn upon turn of the red road he passed, and then stopped, halted by a sight. A sight which for weeks past he had worn in his heart, but which he had never hoped to see fulfilled. She was there, that child! That child so young, so voluptuous in her development, so immature in her mentality, and beside her, a little way away, sat the Kling prisoner who guarded her. The Kling squatted upon his heels, chewing areca nut, and spitting long distances before him. The child also squatted upon the grass by the roadside, very listless. The Kling did not move as Mercier approached, clapping in his sandals. But the child moved and cast upon him a luminous, frightened gaze, and then regarded him fixedly. Therefore Mercier sat down by the child, and noted her. Noted her with a hungry feeling, taking in every beautiful detail. Her exquisite little hands, and her exquisite little feet, shod in wooden sandals, with a button between the toes, such sandals as he was wearing. He talked to her a little, and she answered in half-shy, frightened tones, but underneath he detected a note of passion—such as he felt for her. She was fourteen years old, you see, and fully developed, partly because she was half-witted, and partly because of these hot temperatures under the Equator.

Thus it befell that every morning Mercier arose early, clad his feet in noisy, clapping sandals, and went out for a walk along the red road underlying the mountain. And every morning, almost by accident, he met the half-witted child with her faithful Kling attendant. And the Kling, squatting down upon his heels, chewed areca nut, and spat widely and indifferently, while Mercier sat down beside the little girl and wondered how long he could stand it—before his control gave way. For she was a little animal, you see, and yearned for him in a sort of fourteen-year-old style, fostered by the intense heat of the Tropics. But Mercier, not yet very long from home, held back—because of certain inhibitions. Sometimes he thought he would ask for her in marriage—which was ridiculous, and showed that life in the Far East, especially in a prison colony, affects the brain. At other times, he thought how very awkward it would be, in such a little, circumscribed community as that, if he did not ask her in marriage. Suppose she babbled—as she might well do. There is no accounting for the feeble-minded. But as the days grew on, madder and wilder he became, earlier and earlier he arose to meet her, to go forth to find her on the red road beneath the mountains. There she was always waiting for him, while the Kling, her attendant, squatted chewing betel nut a little farther on.

*　*　*　*　*

In time, he had enough. He had had quite enough. She was a stupid fool, half-witted. He grew quite satiated. Also she grew alarmed. Very much alarmed. But always, in the distance, with his back discreetly turned, sat her Kling guardian, the paroled prisoner, chewing betel nut. So his way out was easy. One day, about eleven o'clock in the morning, clad in very immaculate white clothes, he came to call upon the child's parents, with a painful duty to perform. He must report what he had seen. When out taking his constitutional, he had seen certain things in an isolated spot of the red road, leading up to the mountains. These paroled prisoners could not be trusted—he had intimated as much weeks ago. Therefore he made his report, his painful report, as compelled by duty. In his pocket was his release—the acceptance of his resignation. His recall from his post. When the boat came in next time—that day, in fact—he would go. But he could not go, with a clear conscience, till he had reported on what he had seen. The Kling—the old, stupid, trusted Kling—stupid to trust a child like that with a servant like that—

So the Kling was hanged next morning, and Mercier sailed away that afternoon, when the little steamer came in. The little colony on the island of prisoners went on with its life as usual. Ah, bah! There was no harm done! She was so very immature! Mercier need not have exacted the life of the Kling servant, after all. He was supersensitive and over-scrupulous. Life in a prison colony in the Far East certainly affects one's judgment.

Ellen Newbold La Motte

CANTERBURY CHIMES

I

The Colonial Bishop lay spread out on his long, rattan chair, idly contemplating the view of the harbour, as seen from his deep, cool verandah. As he lay there, pleasant thoughts crossed his mind, swam across his consciousness in a continuous stream, although, properly speaking, he was not thinking at all. The thoughts condensed in patches, were mere agglomerations of feelings and impressions, and they strung themselves across his mind as beads are strung along a string. His mental fingers, however, slipped the beads along, and he derived an impression of each bead as it passed before his half closed eyes. The first that appeared was a sense of physical well-being. He liked the climate. This climate of the Far Eastern Tropics, which so few people could stand, much less enjoy. But he liked it; he liked its enclosing sense of warmth and dampness and heavy scented atmosphere. Never before had he brought such an appetite to his meals, or so enjoyed his exercise, or revelled in perspiration after a hard bicycle ride, and so enjoyed the cool wash and splash in the Java jar afterwards. The climate suited him admirably. It made one very fit, physically, and was altogether delightful. From this you will see that the Bishop was a young man, not over forty-five.

Then the servants. Good boys he had, well trained, obedient, anticipative, amusing, picturesque in their Oriental dress. Rather trying because of their laziness, but not too exasperating to be a real irritant. So many people found native servants a downright source of annoyance—even worse than the climate—but for himself, he had never found them so. They gave him no trouble at all, and he had been out ten years, so ought to know.

The native life was charming too, so rich in colour, in all its gay costumes. Surely the first Futurists must have been the Orientals. No modern of the most ultra-modern school had ever revelled in such gorgeous colour combinations, in such daring contrasts and lurid extremes, as did these dark hued people, in their primitive simplicity. He liked them all, decent and docile. He liked their earrings—only that day he had counted a row of nine in the ear of some wandering juggler. Nose rings too—how pretty they were, nose rings. Rubies too, and most of them real, doubtless. How well they looked in the nostril of a thin, aquiline brown nose. It all went with the country. Barbaric, perhaps, contrasted with other standards, but beautiful—in its way. He would not change it for the world.

And the perfumes! A faint scent of gardenias was at that moment being wafted in from his well-kept, rich gardens, where somehow his boys managed to make flowers grow in the brown, devitalised earth. For the soil was devitalised, surely. It got no rest, year in, year out. For centuries it had nourished, in one long, eternal season, the great rich mass of tropical vegetation. European flowers would not grow in the red earth, or the black earth, whichever it was—he had been accustomed to think of red or black earth as being rich, but out here in the Tropics, it was unable to produce, for more than a brief season, the flowers and shrubs that were native to his home land. But gardenias and frangipanni—

The next bead that slipped along was the memory of an Arab street at dusk—the merchants sitting at their shop fronts, the gloom of the little, narrow shops, the glow of rich stuffs and rich colours that lay in neat piles on the shelves, and the scent of incense burning in little earthenware braziers at the door of each shop—how sweet was the warm air, laden with this deeply sweet smell of burning, glowing incense—

A step sounded on the verandah, and the Bishop concluded his revery abruptly. It was not the nearly noiseless step of a bare foot, such as his servants. It was the step of someone in European shoes, yet without the firm, decided tramp of a European. Yet the tread of a European shoe, muffled to the slithering, soft effect of a native foot. A naked foot, booted. This was the Bishop's hour of rest, and his servants had instructions to admit no one. Well, no one in a general sense, yet there were always two or three recognised exceptions. But it was not one of these exceptions, coming in noiselessly like that. The Bishop sprang up, standing straddle of his long chair, and looking fixedly in the direction of the approaching sound. He hated interruptions, and was indignant to think that any one should have slipped in, past the eyes of his watchful servants. Just then a figure appeared at the far end of the verandah, a white clad figure rapidly advancing. A dark skinned, slim figure, clad in white linen European clothes, even down to a pair of new, ill fitting, white canvas shoes with rubber soles. That accounted for the sound resembling bare feet. Really, they could never wear shoes properly, these natives, however much they might try.

Still standing straddle across his chair, the Bishop called out angrily to the intruder. Since he was not a European, and obviously not a native Prince—native princes never slithered in like that, all the pomp of the East heralded their coming—the Bishop could afford to let his annoyance manifest itself in his voice. Therefore he called out sharply, asking the stranger's business.

A slim youth stepped forward, bare headed, hollow chested, very dark in the gathering twilight, and his hands clasped together as if in supplication, stood out blackly against the whiteness of his tunic. The Bishop noticed that they were trembling. Well they might, for he had taken a great liberty, by this presumptuous, unannounced visit. It had a sort of sneaking character about it. Coming to steal, perhaps, and being surprised in the act, had determined to brazen it out under the pretext of a visit. The young man, however, walked boldly up to the Bishop's chair, and the Bishop, rather taken aback, sat himself down again and extended his legs on the rest, in their usual comfortable position.

"I've come to see you, Sir," began the stranger, using very good English though with a marked native accent, "on a question of great importance. On a matter of principle—of high principle. I've never seen you before, but you are known to me by reputation."

The Bishop snorted at this piece of impudence, but the youth went on unabashed.

"A very noble reputation, if I may presume to say so. But you know that, of course. What you are, what you stand for. Therefore I have dared to come to you for help. It is not a matter of advice—that does not enter in at all. But I want your great help—on our side. To right a great, an immense, an immensely growing wrong."

The youth hesitated and stopped, wringing his dark, thin hands together in evident agitation. The Bishop surveyed him coldly, with curiosity, without sympathy, enjoying his embarrassment. So that was it—some grievance, real or fancied. Fancied, most likely. He felt a distinct sense of resentment that his hour of repose should have been broken in upon so rudely by this native—bringing him wrongs to redress in this uncalled for manner. There were plenty of people in the Bishop's service expressly appointed for the purpose of looking into complaints and attending to them. To bring them up to headquarters, to the Bishop himself, was an act of downright impertinence. Very much as if a native should bring his petty quarrels up to the Governor-General. These thoughts passed through the Bishop's mind as he regarded the intruder with a fixed and most unfriendly eye. A few moments of hesitating silence followed, while the Bishop watched the darting movements of a lizard on the wall, and waited for the stranger to continue.

"I want your help," went on the youth in a low voice. "You are so powerful—you can do so much. Not as a man, but because of your office. Perhaps as a man, too, for they say you are a good and just man. But the combination of a strong man in a high office—"

Still no help from the Bishop. That he did not clap his hands together and call for his servants to have this intruder thrown out, marked him, in his estimation, as the kind of man that the youth had suggested. A just and liberal man. Very well, he was ready to listen. Now that he was caught, so to speak, and obliged to listen against his will.

"It's about the opium traffic," explained the young man, breathing hard with excitement, and wringing his thin hands together in distress.

"Oh, that's it, is it?" exclaimed the Bishop, breaking silence. "I thought it must be some such thing. I mean, something that is no concern of mine—nor yours either," he concluded sharply.

"It is both my concern and your concern," replied the young man solemnly, "both yours and mine. Your race, your country, is sinning against my race and my country—"

"Your country!" interrupted the Bishop disdainfully.

"Yes, my country!" exclaimed the young man proudly. "Mine still, for all that you have conquered it, and civilized it and degraded it!"

The Bishop sprang up from his chair angrily, and then sank back again, determined to listen. He would let this fellow say all he had to say, and then have him arrested afterwards. He would let him condemn himself out of his own mouth. How well they spoke English too, these educated natives.

"What is this Colony, Sir," continued the young man gaining control of himself, "but a market for the opium your Government sells? For you know, Sir, as well as I, that the sale of opium is a monopoly of your Government. And we are helpless, defenceless, powerless to protect ourselves. And do you know what your Government makes out of this trade, Sir—the revenue it collects from selling opium to my people? Three quarters of the revenue of this Colony are derived from opium. Your Government runs this colony on our degradation. You build your roads, your forts, your schools, your public buildings, on this vice that you have forced upon us. Before you came, with your civilization, we were decent. Very decent, on the whole. Now look at us—what do you see? How many shops in this town are licensed by your Government for the sale of opium—and the license money pocketed as revenue? How many opium divans, where we may smoke, are licensed by your Government, and the license money pocketed as part of the revenue?"

"You needn't smoke unless you wish to," remarked the Bishop drily. "We don't force you to do it. We don't put the pipe between your teeth and insist upon your drugging yourselves. How many shops do you say there are—how many smoking places? Several hundred? We don't force you into them, I take it. You go of your own choice, don't you? We Europeans don't do it. It's as free for us as it is for you. We have the same opportunities to kill ourselves—I suppose that's how you look at it—as you do. Yet somehow we abstain. If you can't resist—"

The Bishop shrugged his shoulders. Yet he rather despised himself for the argument. It sounded cheap and unworthy, somehow. The youth, however, did not seem to resent it, and went on sadly.

"It's true," he said, "we need not, I suppose. Yet you know," he continued humbly, "we are a very simple people. We are very primitive, very—lowly. We didn't understand at first, and now it's too late. We've most of us got the habit, and the rest are getting it. We're weak and ignorant. We want you to protect

Ellen Newbold La Motte

us from ourselves. Just as you protect your own people—at home. You don't import it into your own country—you don't want to corrupt your own people. But what about the races you colonise and subject—who can't protect themselves? It's not fair!" he concluded passionately, "and besides, this year you have sold us two millions more than last year—"

"Where did you get your figures?" broke in the Bishop with rising indignation. This cowering, trembling boy seemed to have all the arguments on his side.

"From your own reports, Sir. Government reports. Compiled by your own officials."

"And how did *you* obtain a Government report?" asked the Bishop angrily. "Spying, eh?"

The young man ignored the insult, and went on patiently. "Some are distributed free, others may be bought at the book shops. There is one lying on your table this moment, Sir."

"Well enough for me," remarked the Bishop, "but how did you come by it?" The sharp eyes had recognised the fat, blue volume buried under a miscellaneous litter of books and pamphlets on a wicker table. A lean finger pointed towards it, and the accusing voice went on.

"There is more than opium in that Report, Sir. Look at the schools. How little schooling do you give us, how little money do you spend for them. We are almost illiterate—yet you have ruled us for many years. How little do you spend on schools, so that you may keep us submissive and ignorant? You know how freely you provide us with opium, so that we may be docile and easy to manage—easy to manage and exploit."

The Bishop sprang up from his chair, making a grasp for the white coat of his tormentor, but the fellow nimbly avoided him, and darted to the other side of the table. It was almost completely dark by this time, and the Bishop could not pursue his guest in the gloom, nor could he reach the bell.

"Are you a Seditionist, Sir? How dare you criticise the Government?" The answer was immediate and unexpected.

"Yes, I criticise the Government—just as I have been criticising it to you. But more in sorrow than in anger. Although in time the anger may come. Therefore that is why I have come to you—for help, before our anger comes. You are a strong man, a just, a liberal man—so I'm told. You hold a high position in the Church maintained by your Government, just as the opium traffic is maintained by your Government. Both are Government monopolies."

In the distance the cathedral chimes rang over the still air—the old, sweet Canterbury chimes, pealing the full round, for it was the hour. Then the hour struck, and both men counted it, mechanically.

"Your salary, Sir—as well as the salaries of the other priests of your established church, out here in this Colony—comes from the established opium trade. Your Canterbury chimes ring out, every fifteen minutes, over the opium dens of the Crown!"

At this supreme insult the Bishop leaped at his tormentor, striking a blow into space. The youth bounded over the low rail of the verandah and disappeared amongst the shrubbery in the darkness.

To say that the Bishop was shaken by this interview is to put it mildly. For he was a good man in his way, and moreover, in a certain restricted sense, a religious one. But he was lazy and not inclined to meddle in affairs that did not concern him. And colonial politics and the management of colonial affairs were certainly not his concern. Nevertheless, the horrible grouping together of facts, as the young Seditionist had grouped them for him, their adroit placing together, with the hideous, unavoidable connection between them, upset him tremendously. He sat on in the darkness trying to think, trying to see

Ellen Newbold La Motte

his way clear, trying to excuse or to justify. He had never thought of these things before, yet he well knew of their existence. All sorts of injustices abounded in civilized states—it was perhaps worse in the colonies. Yet even in the colonies, little by little they were being weeded out, or adjusted. Yet this particular evil, somehow, seemed to flourish untouched. Not an effort was made to uproot it. The only effort made, apparently, was to increase and encourage it. And with the acquiescence of men like himself. All for what—for money? For Crown revenues! Pretty poor business, come to think of it. Surely, if the Colony could not exist by honest and legitimate trade, it might better not exist at all. To thrive upon the vices of a subject people, to derive nearly the whole revenue from those vices, really, somehow, it seemed incompatible with— with—that nasty fling about the Church!

He rang for his boy, and a lamp was brought in and placed upon the table beside him, and the Bishop reached over for the unheeded Report, which had been lying on the table so long. The columns of figures seemed rather formidable—he hated statistics, but he applied himself to the Report conscientiously. Yes, there it was in all its simplicity of crude, bald statements, just as the young man had said. Glaring, horrible facts, disgraceful facts. For an hour he sat absorbed in them, noting the yearly increase in consumption as indicated by the yearly increase in revenue. Three quarters of the revenue from opium—one quarter from other things. He wondered vaguely about his salary; that painful allusion to it troubled him. It was just possible that it came from the one quarter derived from legitimate trade. Certainly, it was quite possible. But on the other hand, there was an unquiet suspicion that perhaps it didn't.

The Bishop moved into the dining room, carrying the fat Blue Book under his arm, and read it carefully during his solitary meal. Those carefully compiled tables, somehow, did not do credit to what he had heretofore been pleased to consider the greatest colonising nation in the world. Were all colonies like that—run on these principles? Yet the Government, apparently, had felt no hesitation in setting forth these facts explicitly. Presumably the Government felt justified. Yet it certainly was not—the word honourable rose to his mind, but he suppressed it at once—however, nothing else suggested itself. Years ago, so many years ago that he had lost count, the Bishop had worked for a time in the East End. He had had clubs and classes, and worked with the young men. He used to know a good deal about certain things, and to feel strongly— But since then he had become prosperous, and a high dignitary in the Church. Something stirred uneasily in the back of his mind, as he dawdled over his dinner and turned the pages of the Blue Book—

Then he went back to the verandah again, and subsided into his long chair. He sat in darkness, for he disliked the night-flying insects of the Tropics, and had a nervous horror of them. Lamps made them worse—brought them in thicker shoals. He gazed out at the twinkling lights of the vessels at anchor in the harbour. There were many ships in the roadway to-night, a sight which would ordinarily have pleased him, but his thoughts were in sharp contrast now to his comfortable, contented thoughts of a few hours ago.

II

The Bishop spent rather a wakeful night, that is, until about two in the morning, at which hour he settled his problem and fell asleep. It finally resolved itself in his mind as a matter for him to let alone. He could not better it, and had not the smallest intention of making a martyr of himself, of resigning his office, or of incurring any of the other disagreeable experiences which beset the path of the moral crusader. No, he could do nothing, for at two o'clock, as we have said, he had arrived at the conclusion that the evil—if such it could be called, since there was considerable doubt on the subject—had reached a magnitude which no single individual could deal with. Whereupon he wisely dismissed the matter from his mind. Not having gone to sleep till late he was considerably annoyed when his China-boy arrived at six with his early tea. This sense of irritation still clung to him when an hour later he sat down on the verandah facing the harbour and began his breakfast. Even after ten years in the Tropics, the Bishop still continued to enjoy bacon and eggs with unabated relish, and these did something, this morning, to mitigate his ill humour. A fresh papaya, with a dozen seeds left in as flavouring, also helped. Finally the boy came in and laid letters by his plate. Home letters, bearing the familiar postmarks, so dear to dwellers in outlying parts of the world. A small Malay kriss, with a handle of ivory and silver and a blade of five waves served as letter opener. The Bishop slit each envelope carefully, and laid the pile back on the table, to be read slowly, with full enjoyment. One by one he went through them, smiling a little, or frowning, as it happened. The mail from Home was early this week—evidently it had come in last evening, although he had not seen the steamer in the roads. All the better—all the more of a surprise.

He stopped suddenly, anxiously, and an open letter in his hand trembled violently. He finished it hurriedly, went through it a second time, and again once more before he could acknowledge its meaning.

"MY DEAR BROTHER" [it began, with a formality about the opening that boded trouble], "I write to you in great distress, but sure that you will respond to the great demand I am about to make upon you, upon all the kindness which you have shown us for these many years. Herbert, your namesake, is in deep trouble—disgrace, I might better say. Never mind the details. They are sufficiently serious, sufficiently humiliating. We have managed to cover it up, to conceal what we can, but for the present at least, or until this blows over, it is impossible for him to remain at home. It has all come about so suddenly, so unexpectedly, that there has been no time to write to you to obtain your consent. But he must leave home at once, and there is no one to whom we can send him except yourself. In his present position, feeling the deep dishonour that he has brought upon himself, upon all of us in fact, we do not dare to send him forth into the world alone. Therefore, without delay, we are sending him to you, feeling sure of your response. Under your guidance and care, with the inestimable benefits that he will derive through the association with such a man as yourself, we hope that he will recover his normal balance. Take him in, do what you can for him for all our sakes. He has always been devoted to you, although it was a lad's devotion—you have not seen him for several years, and he is now twenty. Put him to work, do whatever you think best for him; we give him entirely into your hands. We turn to you in this hour of our distress, knowing that you will not fail us.

"Such is the urgency, that he is going out to you on the boat that carries this letter. Failing that, he will leave in any event on the boat of the following week. We regret that there has not been sufficient time to prepare you. He will be no expense, being well provided with funds, although in future I shall make out his remittances in your name. In haste, in grief, and with all love,

"Your affectionate brother,
"ALLAN."

The Bishop sat thunderstruck in his chair, aghast at his predicament. Here was a pretty situation! A scapegrace nephew, who had done heavens knew what dishonourable thing—the Bishop thought of a dozen things all at once, all equally disgraceful and equally probable,—was about to be quartered upon him, in his peaceful, ordered, carefree life, for an indefinite period! Really, it was intolerable. What did he, the Bishop, know of young men and their difficulties? Who was he to guide the footsteps of an erring one? What practical experience had he in such matters—it was one thing to expound certain niceties of theological doctrine, which, after all, had little bearing on daily life—and quite another to become guardian and preceptor to a young scamp. For he was a scamp, obviously. And of all places in the world, to send a weak, undisciplined person out to the Colony—this rather notorious Colony where even those of the highest principles had some difficulty in holding to the path. It was obvious that the place for this young man was in his home—in the home of his father and mother, who while they had doubtless spoiled him, must nevertheless retain a certain influence. He needed all the kindness and loving care that a home could give. The Bishop sought refuge in platitudes, for of such consisted his daily thoughts, running through his brain in certain well defined, well worn brain paths. Then a wave of indignation passed over him concerning his brother—the selfishness of turning his son out, at this time of all times! Of shirking responsibility towards him, of turning that responsibility over to another! To another whom he had not even consulted! All his life his brother had had what he wanted—riches, a beautiful home, an easy life. Yet at the first breath of trouble he evaded his responsibilities and dumped them upon another!

The Bishop worked himself up into a fine fury, seeing his future plans upset, his easy-going life diverted from its normal, flowing course by the advent of this scapegrace nephew. His eyes rested once more upon the letter: "He is going out to you on the boat that carries this letter." If so, then he must have already landed and would appear at any moment. For the mailboat must have come in last night, and the passengers had either been put ashore last evening, or had been put ashore at sunrise, supposing the boat remained discharging cargo all night. It was now eight o'clock. The youth should have been here. Apparently, then, he had failed to catch this boat, and was coming the following week. But the Bishop was troubled; he must go into town and make sure. Since he was to be burdened with the rascal for a week (but only for a week, he would send him packing home by the next boat, he promised himself) his sense of duty prompted him to act at once. He raised his fine, thin hands and clapped them together smartly.

"Rickshaw! Quickly!" he ordered the China-boy who appeared in answer to his summons. A few minutes later he descended the broad steps of the verandah and entered his neat, black rickshaw, with highly polished brasses, drawn by two boys in immaculate white livery. The Bishop kept no carriage—that would have seemed ostentatious—but his smart, black rickshaw was to be seen all over town, stopping before houses of high and low degree, but mostly high.

He reached the quais after a sharp run, passing the godowns filled with rubber, which gave forth its peculiar, permeating odour upon the heavy, stagnant air of the harbourside. No, the mailboat had gone on, had weighed anchor early in the morning, at sunrise, they told him, and had continued on her way up the coast. No such passenger as he described had been landed—no one by that name. The Bishop, leaning upon the worn counter in the dingy shipping office, scrutinised the passenger list carefully. There was a name there, certainly, that suggested his nephew's, but with two or three wrong letters. Not enough for a positive identification, but perhaps done purposely, as a disguise. Could the youth have deliberately done this? It was possible. When pressed for a description, the Bishop was most hazy. He could only say that he was searching for a young man, about twenty. The agent told him that twenty young men, about twenty, had come ashore. The Bishop was not quite satisfied, was vaguely uneasy, but there was nothing to be done. However, when the day passed and no nephew appeared, he drew a long breath of relief. He was safe

Ellen Newbold La Motte

for another week. Had a week before him in which to formulate his plans. And he would formulate them too, he promised himself, and would put the responsibility of this irresponsible young creature back upon the shoulders where it belonged. It was a great temptation not to return to the shipping office again and engage a berth on the next homeward bound liner, but on second thought, he determined not to do so. Above all things he prided himself on being just and liberal. He would give his nephew a week's trial in the Colony, after which the letter returning him to his father would bear the air of resigned but seasoned judgment, rather than the unreasoning impulse of a moment's irritation. A week's guardianship, and—well, so it should be. Nothing longer, no greater incursion into his smooth, harmonious existence.

The week of anticipation passed slowly. After the first shock was over, after the first sense of imposition had passed away, and he found himself with a week for consideration, he became more decided than ever on his course of action. Mentally, he began many letters to his brother, usually beginning, "I regret exceedingly," from which beginning he launched out into well balanced, well phrased excuses, of admirable logic, by means of which he proved the imperative necessity of finding other anchorage for this stray and apparently very frail bark. Of necessity these letters were vague, since he did not know what particular form of frailty he had to contend with. Of one thing, however, he was sure—the Colony offered opportunities for the indulgence of every form known to man, with none of those nice restrictions which are thrown round such opportunities in more civilized parts of the globe. He would explain all this at length, as soon as he knew upon which points to concentrate his argument. But, take it by and large, there were no safeguards of any sort, and only the strongest and most upright could walk uprightly amidst such perils.

The coming of the next liner was awaited with much anxiety. The Bishop had gone so far as to confide to a few friends that a young nephew would arrive with her, for a week's stay—on his way elsewhere. He remembered the boy, his namesake. Rather a handsome little chap as he recalled him—perhaps under more auspicious circumstances it might have been a pleasure to have had a visit from him. But this suddenly becoming endowed with him for weeks or months—it might be years, perhaps—quite another matter.

When the mailboat arrived one afternoon, the Bishop's rickshaw stood at the jetty, while the Bishop himself, in his immaculate gaiters, with his sash blowing in the soft wind, stood at the end of the jetty anxiously regarding the tender making its way inshore. She was crowded with a miscellaneous throng of passengers, among whom were many young men, all strange, new, expectant young men coming out for the first time, but among them he saw no face that resembled the one he was searching for. Which might possibly be, he reflected, since the face, as he recalled it at the time of their last meeting many years ago, was very childish and immature. The tender made fast to the steps, and amidst much luggage, much scrambling of coolies and general disorder, the passengers came off. The Bishop standing on the steps scrutinised each one carefully. Not there. Nor was there a second trip to the liner, since the tender had fetched ashore all who were to disembark at that port. The Bishop turned away with mingled feelings, part relief, part indignation. Another week of suspense to be gone through with, and after that, another week before he could release himself of his burden. It was all exceedingly trying and unreasonable—the feeling of irritation against his brother mounted higher—it was outrageous, keeping him upset this way.

Then a thought suddenly came into his mind. That name on the passenger list a week ago, the name slightly different yet curiously alike—could it have been altered slightly on purpose? Ashamed to face him, ashamed to come to him? Bundled off in disgrace from home, willy-nilly, and now here,—hiding?

A wave of sick apprehension came over the Bishop. Agonising

fear. He must see Walker at once. Walker, his old friend, who would know what to do, what to advise. If only he were in town.

Walker was in town as it happened, and the Bishop found him at his hotel, and poured out to him all his wretched anxieties, the whole miserable business, not sparing himself in describing his attitude of unwelcome and unwillingness to receive the boy, and concluding with his sick fears concerning his safety. Walker listened gravely and attentively, and was troubled. It was very possible indeed—more than possible. A search must be begun at once. Fortunately, in that small community, it was not easy for a foreigner to disappear, and a stranger could not go inland, into the interior, undetected. Therefore, if he was here at all, he would soon be found—somewhere. He would set in motion the machinery immediately. First the hotels; that was easy. Then the other places. It would doubtless be necessary to call in the police.

The Bishop begged for secrecy—no publicity. Walker promised. That, too, would be easy. Leave it to him. The Bishop might rest easy on that score—no publicity. Walker would do everything himself, as far as possible. Only, he might have to send for the Bishop, if it became necessary, to identify—

Two nights later, the Bishop was reclining on the long chair on his verandah, while overhead the heavy punkah fans swayed to and fro, stirring the moist, warm air. Out in the harbour the lights gleamed fitfully, the lanterns on the bobbing sampans contrasting with the steadier beams of the big ships anchored in the roadway. The ships of the Orient, congregated from the Seven Seas, full of the mystery and romance of the East. He had left it to Walker—as he had been told. In the darkness, with one hand clasped behind his head and the other holding a glowing cigar, he contemplated the scene, his favourite hour of the day. Each moment another and another light flitted across the heavy blackness, showing red or green, while the lights on the moving sampans darted back and forth in the darkness, restless and alert. He had left it to Walker. He had stopped thinking of his impending nephew for a few moments, and his mind had relaxed, as the mind relaxes when an evil has been postponed from time to time, and normal feeling reasserts itself after the reprieve. There was a quiet footfall on the verandah, and the Bishop was aroused from his meditations. His Chinese servant approached deferentially. "Man want see Master," he explained laconically, with the imperturbability of the East.

"What like man?" enquired the Bishop, in pidgin English. "China man," came the response. "Must see Master. All belong velly important."

A quick foreboding possessed the Bishop, even in this hour of his tranquillity.

"Show him here," he replied, after a second's consideration. A tall figure appeared before him, bowing. A lean, very dirty Chinese, who bowed repeatedly. In spite of the Oriental repression of feeling, it was plain that he was troubled. He extended a lean, claw-like hand, with a long and very dirty nail on the little finger, and offered a soiled letter to the Bishop.

"Velly important. All belong much tlouble," he explained, and tucked his hands well inside his long blue sleeves, and stood by impassively, while the Bishop received the letter, crumpled and soiled, as if carried for a long time in a pocket. He turned it over and found it addressed to himself. There was no stamp. The handwriting was Walker's. The Bishop started erect in his long chair, and then sprang up, straddling it as usual.

"Where get this?" he asked excitedly. The impassive Chinese bowed once more.

"Say come quick. Letter velly important. Letter belong you. No police. My savee you want letter now." He backed away, still bowing. With a sweep of his arm he indicated the dark night outside.

"You come quick," he repeated, "or call police." By the light of a lamp which his obsequious but curious Chinese servant carried in, the Bishop tore open Walker's letter, read it, then crushed it hurriedly into his pocket.

"Come quick," reiterated the unknown Chinese, "I got lickshaw." The Bishop strode forward across the verandah, snatching at his hat as he went, and then hastened across the lawn with hurried steps, followed by the Chinese pacing rapidly behind him. Two rickshaws were waiting under the street lamp, two shabby rickshaws. Yet somehow, the Bishop did not care for his own private conveyance at this moment, did not wish the sharp, inquisitive eyes of his runners to follow him just then. He mounted hastily, and the coolies started off with a will, the Chinese leading the way. Even in that moment of anxiety, the Bishop was aware that the Chinese was leading the way, was conscious that the place of honour was not his— for the first time in his life, his vehicle followed, second place, a rickshaw that carried a Chinese.

The distance seemed interminable. Fortunately, at that hour few of his acquaintances were abroad, but in the anxiety which possessed him, he scarcely realised it. He was conscious of passing through crowded streets, the quarter of the Mohammedans, where incense pots were alight, scenting the warm air. Then the vile-smelling bazaar, crowded with buyers, bargaining and shouting under the swaying torches. Then they passed the European section of the town, where the streets were wide, clean and deserted. They must be going back of the quais now, for the air was heavy with the acrid scent of rubber. Then they turned into a narrow, wildly tumultuous street full of Chinese, scattered all over the road and sidewalk, shouting, calling, beating drums, yelling wares for sale, the babel of the Chinese quarter, only such as the Bishop had never seen it. The rickshaws turned many times, up narrow lanes and alleys, across wider thoroughfares, and finally halted before a dingy house of many storeys, a foreign-style house, converted to native uses. They stopped before a red painted door, a double door, in two halves, like a saloon door. Over the entrance hung a sign, black and white, in large, sprawling Chinese characters. Subconsciously, he was aware that he had passed such signs, in such characters, many times before. A curious and large crowd gathered before the house parted at their approach, and the filthy Chinese led the way, followed by the Bishop in his immaculate garb. As they passed in and the swing doors closed behind them, a throng of yellow faces peered down and looked under the door, which was hung high. And all the while, the low, insistent shuffling noises of the crowd outside penetrated into the dark, dimly lit room in which the Bishop and his companion found themselves.

Around three sides of this room, which was narrow, ran a wide bench covered with dirty matting. Lying at intervals in pairs all along the bench, were two coolies in a little pen, with a lamp between them, separated by a narrow ridge from the pen adjoining, which held two more ragged smokers. The Bishop beheld rows of them, haggard, pallid rows. A horn lantern was suspended from the ceiling, and the air was unstirred by punkah, the heavy, foul air reeking with the sickening, pungent fumes of opium. As he passed, the smokers raised themselves on their elbows and gazed at him with glazed, dull eyes. The sight of a Bishop in a low class opium den was unusual, and the dimmed brains of the smokers dimly recognised the distraction. Then, as he moved on, they sank down again upon their wooden pillows, and with slow, infinite pains, set themselves to roll their bits of opium, to cook it over the dim lamps that dotted the murky atmosphere with glints of light, and to resume their occupations.

At the back of the room, the proprietor paused before a part of the bench where the pen was occupied by one smoker only, a foreigner. The foreigner lay stretched out in an awkward attitude, knees drawn up, his head sliding off the wooden block, most uncomfortable. A candle was thrust into the Bishop's unsteady hand.

"Looksee," whispered a voice. The Bishop looked. "All lite?" questioned the anxious voice of the proprietor, "Die lil' while ago. No can smoke like China boys. No can do."

The Bishop continued to look at the beautiful, disdainful head of the young foreigner, sliding limply off its wooden pillow.

"All lite?" continued the whining voice insistently. "My got money. Have got watch. No steal." A skinny hand with filthy fingernails crept forth and thrust itself into the pockets of the limp waistcoat, crumpled so pitifully upon the thin, young figure, and presently a gold watch was drawn forth. The watch was slowly waved before the Bishop's eyes, and the case snapped open, so that he could read the name engraved within. After which the Bishop continued to gaze fixedly upon the dead youth, lying disgraced upon a bench in one of the lowest opium dives in the Colony.

"Smoke here week," went on the insistent voice of the proprietor, "all time smoke. No go out. No eat. Smoke all same China-boy. No same China-boy. No can do."

There was a slight movement at the back of the room, and an object was passed from hand to hand and finally held for inspection under the Bishop's nose. In a grimy frame, protected by a square of fly-brown glass, was a square, official-looking bit of paper. Of value evidently, since much care had been taken to preserve it.

"License," went on the explanatory voice. "Gov'ment license. All samee Gov'ment license. Pay heap money. No can help if man die. Plenty China-boy die too. This velly lespectable place."

The Bishop recalled himself as from a dream. During the few moments he had spent looking down upon the huddled figure, he seemed to have grown older, to have shrunken down, to have lost something of his fine, arrogant hearing and conscious superiority.

"All lite?" whined the voice insistently. "All lite?" "Yes," said the Bishop shortly, "it's all right." He strode rapidly through the foul room, through the heavy, tainted, pungent air. Outside, the dense crowd pressed closely about the swinging doors scattered widely as he approached. Two policemen were coming down the street, attracted by the excitement of the crowd. The Bishop got into a rickshaw and drove homewards. A heavy weight seemed to have been lifted from his mind. Through the oppressive, hot night air the Canterbury chimes pealed their mellow notes.

"Thank God," said the Bishop fervently, "it was not *my* nephew."

Ellen Newbold La Motte

UNDER A WINEGLASS

A little coasting steamer dropped anchor at dawn at the mouth of Chanta-Boun creek, and through the long, hot hours she lay there, gently stirring with the sluggish tide, waiting for the passage-junk to come down from Chanta-Boun town, twelve miles further up the river. It was stifling hot on the steamer, and from side to side, whichever side one walked to, came no breeze at all. Only the warm, enveloping, moist heat closed down, stifling. Very quiet it was, with no noises or voices from the after deck, where under the awning lay the languid deck passengers, sleeping on their bedding rolls. Very quiet it was ashore, so still and quiet that one could hear the bubbling, sucking noises of the large land-crabs, pattering over the black, oozy mud, or the sound of a lean pig scratching himself against the piles of a native hut, the clustered huts, mounted on stilts, of the village at the mouth of the creek.

The Captain came down from the narrow bridge into the narrow saloon. He was clad in yellow pajamas, his bare feet in native sandals, and held a well pipeclayed topee in one hand. Impatient he was at the delay of the passage-junk coming down from up-river, with her possible trifling cargo, and possible trifling deck-passengers, of which the little steamer already carried enough.

"This long wait—it is very annoying," he commented, sitting upon the worn leather cushions of the saloon bench. "And I had wished for time enough to stop to see the lonely man. I have made good time on this trip—all things considered. With time to spare, to make that call, out of our way. And now the good hours go by, while we wait here, uselessly."

"The lonely man?" asked the passenger, who was not a deck-passenger. He was the only saloon passenger, and because of that, he slept first in one, then in the other of the two small cabins, alternating according to which side the wind blew from.

"You would not mind, perhaps," continued the Captain, "if, after all—in spite of this long delay—we still found time for the lonely man? An unscheduled call, much out of our way—oh, a day's sail from here, and we, as you know, go slowly—"

"Three days from now—four days from now—it matters little to me when we reach Bangkok," said the passenger largely, "but tell me of this man."

Upon the sideboard, under an inverted wineglass, sat a small gilt Buddha, placed there by the China-boys. The Captain fixed his eyes upon the Buddha.

"Like that. Immovable and covered in close, sitting still in a small space. Covered in. Some one turned a wineglass over on him, long ago, and now he sits, still and immovable like that. It makes my heart ache."

"Tell me. While we are waiting."

"Three years ago," began the Captain dreamily, still looking at the tiny gilt Buddha in its inverted wineglass, "he came aboard. Bound for nowhere in particular—to Bangkok, perhaps, since we were going that way. Or to any other port he fancied along the coast, since we were stopping all along the coast. He wanted to lose himself, he said. And, as you have seen, we stop at many remote, lonely villages, such as this one. And we have seen many lonely men, foreigners, isolated in villages such as this one, unknown, removed, forgotten. But none of them suited him. He had been looking for the proper spot for many years. Wandering up and down the coast, in cargo-boats, in little coasting vessels, in sailing vessels, sometimes in native junks, stopping here and there, looking for a place where he could go off and live by himself. He wanted to be quite, absolutely, to himself. He said he should know the place immediately, if he saw it—recognise it at once. He said he could find himself if he could get quite absolutely away. Find himself, that is, recover himself—something, a part of him which he had lost. Just temporarily lost. He was very wistful and very eager, and said I must not think him a fool, or demented. He said he only wanted to be by himself, in the right spot, to accomplish his purpose. He would accomplish his purpose and then return.

"Can you see him, the lonely man, obsessed, going up and down the China Coast, shipping at distant ports, one after another, on fruitless quests, looking for a place to disembark. The proper place to disembark, the place which he should recognise, should know for his own place, which would answer the longing in him which had sent him searching round the world, over the Seven Seas of the world. The spot in which he could find himself again and regain what he had lost.

"There are many islands hereabouts," went on the Captain. "Hundreds. Desert. He thought one would suit him. So I put him down on one, going out of my way to find it for him. He leaned over the rail of the bridge, and said to me 'We are getting nearer.' Then he said that he saw it. So I stopped the ship and put him down. He was very grateful. He said he liked to be in the Gulf of Siam. That the name had a picturesque sound, the Pirate Islands. He would live all by himself on one of the Pirate Islands, in the Gulf of Siam. Isolated and remote, but over one way was the coast of Indo-China, and over the other way was the coast of Malay. Neighbourly, but not too near. He should always feel that he could get away when he was ready, what with so much traffic through the Gulf, and the native boats now and then. He was mistaken about the traffic, but I did not tell him so. I knew where he was and could watch him. I placed a cross on the chart, on his island, so that I might know where I had left him. And I promised myself to call upon him, from time to time—to see when he should be ready to face the world again."

The Captain spread a chart upon the table.

"Six degrees north latitude," he remarked, "Ten thousand miles from—"

"Greenwich," supplied the passenger, anxious to show that he knew.

"From Her," corrected the Captain.

"He told me about her a little. I added the rest, from what he omitted. It all happened quite a long time ago, which was the bother of it. And because it had taken place so long ago, and had endured for so long a time, it made it more difficult for him to recover himself again. Do you think people ever recover themselves again? When the precious thing in them, the spirit of them has been overlaid and overlaid, covered deep with artificial layers—?

"The marvel was that he wanted to regain it—wanted to break through. Most don't. The other thing is so easy. Money—of course. She had it, and he loved her. He had none, and she loved him. She had had money always, had lived with it, lived on it, it got into her very bones. And he had not two shillings to rub together, but he possessed the gift—genius. But they met somewhere, and fell in love with each other, and that ended him. She took him, you see, and gave him all she had. It was marvellous to do it, for she loved him so. Took him from his four shilling attic into luxury. Out of his shabby, poor, worn clothes into the best there were. From a penny 'bus into superb motors. With all the rest of it to match. And he accepted it all because he loved her, and it was the easiest way. Besides, just before she had come into his life, he had written—well, whatever it was—however, they all praised him, the critics and reviewers, and called him the coming man, and he was very happy about it, and she seemed to come into his life right at the top of his happiness over his work. And sapped it. Didn't mean to, but did. Cut his genius down at the root. Said his beginning fame was quite enough—quite enough for her, for her friends, for the society into which she took him. They all praised him without understanding how great he was, or considering his future. They took him at her valuation, which was great enough. But she thought he had achieved the summit. Did not know, you see, that there was anything more.

"He was so sure of himself, too, during those first few years. Young and confident, conscious of his power. Drifting would not matter for a while. He could afford to drift. His genius would ripen, he told himself, and time was on his side. So he drifted, very happy and content, ripening. And being overlaid all the time, deeper and thicker, with this intangible, transparent, strong wall, hemming him in, shutting in the gold, just like that little joss there under the wineglass.

"She lavished on him everything, without measure. But she had no knowledge of him, really. Just another toy he was, the best of all, in her luxurious equipment. So he travelled the world with her, and dined at the Embassies of the world, East and West, in all the capitals of Europe and of Asia. Getting restive finally, however, as the years wore on. Feeling the wineglass, as it were, although he could not see it. Looking through its clear transparency, but feeling pressed, somehow, conscious of the closeness. But he continued to sit still, not much wishing to move, to stretch himself.

"Then sounds from the other side began to filter in, echoing largely in his restricted space, making within it reverberations that carried vague uneasiness, producing restlessness. He shifted himself within his space, and grew conscious of limitations. From without came the voices, insistent, asking what he was doing now? Meaning, what thing was he writing now, for a long time had passed since he had written that which called forth the praise of men. There came to him, within his wineglass, these demands from the outside.

Therefore he grew very uneasy, and tried to rise, and just then it was that he began to feel how close the crystal walls surrounded him. He even wanted to break them, but a pang at heart told him that was ingratitude. For he loved her, you see. Never forget that.

"Now you see how it all came about. He was conscious of himself, of his power. And while for the first years he had drifted, he was always conscious of his power. Knew that he had but to rise, to assume gigantic stature. And then, just because he was very stiff, and the pain of stiffness and stretching made him uncouth, he grew angry. He resented his captivity, chafed at his being limited like that, did not understand how it had come about. It had come about through love. Through sheer, sheltering love. The equivalent of his for her. She had placed a crystal cup above him, to keep him safe. And he had sat safe beneath it all these years, fearing to stir, because she liked him so.

"It came to a choice at last. His life of happiness with her—or his work. Poor fool, to have made the choice at that late day. So he broke his wineglass, and his heart and her heart too, and came away. And then he found that he could not work, after all. Years of sitting still had done it.

"At first he tried to recover himself by going over again the paths of his youth. A garret in London, a studio off Montparnasse, shabby, hungry—all no use. He was done for. Futile. Done himself in for no purpose, for he had lost her too. For you see he planned, when he left her, to come back shortly, crowned anew. To come back in triumph, for she was all his life. Nothing else mattered. He just wanted to lay something at her feet, in exchange for all she had given him. Said he would. So they parted, heart-broken, crushed, neither one understanding. But he promised to come back, with his laurels.

"That parting was long ago. He could not regain himself. After his failure along the paths of his youth, his garrets and studios, he tried to recover his genius by visiting again all the parts of the world he had visited with her. Only this time, humbly. Standing on the outside of palaces and Embassies, recollecting the times when he had been a guest within. Rubbing shoulders with the crowd outside, shabby, poor, a derelict. Seeking always to recover that lost thing.

"And getting so impatient to rejoin her. Longing for her always. Coming to see that she meant more to him than all the world beside. Eating his heart out, craving her. Longing to return, to reseat himself under his bell. Only now he was no longer gilded. He must gild himself anew, bright, just as she had found him. Then he could go back.

"But it could not be done. He could not work. Somewhere in the world, he told me, was a spot where he could work. Where there were no memories. Somewhere in the Seven Seas lay the place. He should know it when he saw it. After so many years' exclusion, he was certain he should feel the atmosphere of the place where he could work. And there he would stay till he finished, till he produced the big thing that was in him. Thus, regilded, he would return to her again. One more effort, once more to feel his power, once more to hear the stimulating rush of praise,—then he would give it up again, quite content to sit beneath his wine-glass till the end. But this first.

"So I put him down where I have told you, on a lonely island. Somewhat north of the Equator, ten thousand miles away from Her. Wistfully, he said it was quite the right spot. He could feel it. So we helped him, the China-boys and I, to build a little hut, up on stilts, thatched with palm leaves. Very desolate it is. On all sides the burnished ocean, hot and breathless. And the warm, moist heat, close around, still and stifling. Like a blanket, dense, enveloping. But he said it was the spot. I don't know. He has been there now three years. He said he could do it there—if ever. From time to time I stop there, if the passengers are willing for a day or two's delay. He looks very old now, and very thin, but he always says it's all right. Soon, very soon now, the manuscript will be ready. Next time I stop, perhaps. Once I came upon him sobbing. Landing early in the morning, slipped ashore and found him sobbing. Head in arms and shoulders shaking. It was early in the morning and I think he'd sobbed all night. Somehow, I think it was not for the gift he'd lost—but for Her.

"But he says over and over again that it is the right spot—the very right place in the world for such as he. Told me that I must not mind, seeing him so lonely, so apparently depressed. That it was nothing. Just the Tropics, and being so far away, and perhaps thinking a little too much of things that did not concern his work. But the work would surely come on. Moods came on him from time to time, which he recognised were quite the right moods in which to work, in which to produce great things. His genius was surely ripe now—he must just concentrate. Some day, very shortly, there would be a great rush, he should feel himself charged again with the old, fine fire. He would produce the great work of his life. He felt it coming on—it would be finished next time I called.

"This is the next time. Shall we go?" asked the Captain.

Accordingly, within a day or two, the small coastwise steamer dropped her anchor in a shallow bay, off a desert island marked with a cross on the Captain's chart, and unmarked upon all other charts of the same waters. All around lay the tranquil spaces of a desolate ocean, and on the island the thatched roof of a solitary hut showed among the palms. The Captain went ashore by himself, and presently, after a little lapse of time, he returned.

"It is finished," he announced briefly, "the great work is finished. I think it must have been completed several weeks ago. He must have died several weeks ago. Possibly soon after my last call."

He held out a sheet of paper on which was written one word, "Beloved."

CHOLERA

There is cholera in the land, and there is fear of cholera in the land. Both are bad, though they are different. Those who get cholera have no fear of it. They are simple people and uneducated, fishermen and farmers, and little tradesmen, and workers of many kinds. Those who have fear of cholera have more intelligence, and know what it means. They have education, and their lives are bigger lives—more imposing, as it were, and they would safeguard them. Those who are afraid are the foreigners and the officials, yes, even the Emperor himself. Is he afraid, the Emperor? One can but guess. He has spent many weeks of this hot summer, when cholera was ravaging his country, in his summer palace at Nikko. There he was safe. And cholera spread itself throughout the land, in the seaports, in the capital, across the rice-fields to the inland villages, taking its toll here and there, of little petty lives. But dangerous to the Emperor, these lives, afflicted or cut short, whichever happens. So he is staying safe at Nikko, in seclusion, waiting for the cool of Autumn to come and purge his land.

Once he was to come back to Tokyo, to his capital. For September waned and he was due there, the Son of Heaven, due in his capital. Many of his subjects came to the station at Nikko on the day appointed for his departure, stepping with short steps in their high clogs, tinkling on the roadside in their clogs, scratching in their sandals. They came in crowds to the station, at the hour when he was due to enter the royaltrain. But when the time came for his departure, he did not go. He would tarry awhile longer at Nikko. So the crowds were disappointed and did not understand. Rumour had it that cholera had developed in the royal household itself—the Purveyor to the Palace, so it was stated, had contracted the disease. A fish dealer, bringing fish to the palace, had brought cholera with him. So the Emperor tarries at Nikko, and the highroad, behind the Imperial Palace in Tokyo is closed to the public, lest any poor coolie, strolling by, should become ill and bring this dread thing near to the precincts of the Son of Heaven.

The foreigners are very careful as to what they eat. They avoid the fruits, the ripe, rich Autumn figs, and the purple grapes, and the hard, round, woody pears, and the sweet butter and many other things. Oh, these days the rich foreigners are very careful of themselves, and meal times are not as pleasant as they used to be. They discuss their food, and wonder about it. And because there is cholera, rife in the ports, and among the fishermen and sailors, the authorities have closed the fish market of Tokyo. The great Nihom-Bashi market, down by the bridge, the vile, evil smelling fish market, lying along the sluggish canal, is closed. The canal is full of straw thatched boats. It all smells very nasty in that quarter, it smells like cholera. No wonder there is cholera, with that smell. No wonder the great market is closed. So the baskets of bamboo are empty, turned upside down, for there is no fish in them. The people, bare-legged, nearly naked, stand idly about the empty fish market, and talk together of this fear which is abroad, which has ruined their trade. What is this fear? They cannot understand. They do not know it. Only the Emperor cannot eat fish now, for some reason, and their business is ruined because of his caprice.

It is very hot. All summer has this great heat continued, and it makes one nervous. Day after day it lasts, unbroken, always the same, unavoidable. There is no escape from the stifling dampness of it—one cannot breathe. Over all the land it is like this, this heavy, sultry heat. It is no cooler when it rains, no dryer when the hot sun shines. It is enveloping, engulfing. In the big hotel, the leather shoes of the foreigners become mouldy overnight, and the sweat runs in streams from the brown bodies of the rickshaw boys. The rickshaw boys of the big hotel wear clothes, long legged, tight cotton trousers, and flapping white coats. This is to save the feelings of the foreigners and the missionaries, who believe that clothing should always be worn, even in hot weather. So as the rickshaw boy runs along, one can see his white coat grow damp between the shoulder blades, then wet all across the back, till it is all wet and sticks to him tight. Yet it is more modest to wear clothes, when doing the work of a horse. One does not object to a man doing the work of a horse, provided he dress like a man. But the coolies toiling at the log carts, and the little tradesmen in their shops, wear few clothes, because they areindependent of the foreigners. Therefore they seem to suffer less with the heat, or to suffer less obviously. Ah, but the heat is intense, overwhelming! Day after day, one cannot breathe. And in it, cholera goes on.

They say a typhoon is coming. Word has come from Formosa that a typhoon is rushing up from the southern seas, from Hong Kong, the Equator, wherever it is they come from. It will reach us to-night. That will be better. The heat will go then, blown from the land by the gigantic blast of the typhoon, zig-zagging up the coast from Formosa. Well, it is late September—this unnatural heat,—why will it not leave? Why must it linger till torn like a blanket from the sweating earth, by this hurricane from the Southern seas?

Only it did not come—the typhoon. They said it would, but it failed. Has it gone shooting off into the Pacific, futile? So the damp, stifling heat lingers, and the toll of cholera rolls slowly upward day by day.

It is a long way from Nikko to Tokyo by motor. A hundred miles, when one can cross the bridge, but the bridge is washed away now, so a detour of many more miles is necessary, to ferry the motor across the Tonegawa on a flat bottomed, frail boat. The motor sinks nearly to the hubs in the blazing, glaring sands of the dry river bed, and many naked coolies are needed to push and pull it through the hot sands, and work it into the boat. In the glaring sun of noon, the broad river lies motionless, like a sheet of glowing steel. Children bathe in the river, and the sweating coolies dip their brown bodies in it, and the sun beats down pitiless. A junk gets loose from its moorings, and drifts down stream, stern first, on the slow current. Who cares? No one. It will beach itself presently, on a mud flat, and can be recovered towards evening. The great heat lies over all the land, and cholera is in the slowly flowing water, and the fishermen and the coolies and the children live and work and play by the river bank, and they have no fear of it, because they are ignorant.

From Nikko to the capital, the road runs through village after village, endlessly, mile after mile. On each side of the village street are straw thatched houses, and along the roads coolies bend under great loads, carried on poles across their shoulders. Black bulls drag giant loads on two wheeled carts, their masters straining beside them. The bulls' mouths are open, their tongues hang out, and saliva drools out in streams. It leaves a wet, irregular wake, in the dust of the roadside, behind the carts. By and by, the men will stop for food and drink. They cannot choose what it shall be. They cannot afford to choose. But the food of the Emperor is carefully selected. Physicians examine those who handle it, who bring it to the Palace, to see that they are in good health. They examine the food, disinfect it, see to its cooking. News of this is in the papers each day, not to show that the Emperor is afraid, but to set an example to his subjects.

In the houses along the roadside, little tradesmen are at work, all naked in the heat. Or else they are bathing. For all along the high road from Nikko to the capital, following its every bend and turning, runs a ditch or channel filled with water. Sometimes the water is clean and rushing, sometimes foul and stagnant and evil smelling. And all the way along the high road people are bathing in this ditch or channel, in the foul or running water, as it happens. They stand naked, knee deep, men and children, while the women wash and bathe also, but more modestly. Also, besides their bodies, they wash much else in this long ditch,—clothes, pots, what-not. Very dirty seems this channel, sewer, bath tub, as you please. And cholera is abroad in the land.

At the entrance to the temples sits the image of Binzuru. Long ago, when history was new and the gods were young, Binzuru, one of the sixteen great disciples, broke his vow of chastity by remarking on the beauty of a woman. So he was put outside the temples. His image no longer rests upon the altars, with those of the calm, serene ones. He's disgraced, expelled, no longer fit to sit upon the altars, with the cold, serene ones, in their colossal calm. He's so human now, outside the temples. Sitting on a chair for human beings to touch him, now he's off the altar, he's in contact with humanity. The devout ones rub his wooden image—there is no bronze or gold in poor Binzuru's makeup. So the people rub his wooden image, rub his ears, his head, his forehead, rub his arms, his legs, his shoulders. How they suffer, human beings! How their bodies ache and suffer, judged by poor Binzuru's body! For if you rub Binzuru on the part which hurts you in your body, and then rub your body with a hand fresh from Binzuru, you will be cured. Your pain will go. That's true. Binzuru is polished smooth and shining, quite deformed with rubbing—his poor head's a nubbin! And in gratitude for what he's done for people, he sits now on a pile of cushions, one for each new cure. Bibs and caps adorn him too, votive offerings from the faithful whom he's cured.

But he is no good for cholera, poor Binzuru. You can't reach him quick enough to rub his stomach, then your own. Cholera's too quick for that. You can't reach him soon enough. He can't help in this.

Down the road a stretcher comes, swinging from a bamboo pole, carried on the shoulders of two men. Over it a mat is thrown, and through the little open triangle at one end, you see a pair of brown legs lying. Only legs, no more. Drawn up stiffly, toes clinched.

Here in the hospital they lie in rows, very quiet. Not an outcry, not a murmur. Everything is swimming in carbolic. The nurses wear masks across their mouths and noses. They come and go in clogs, barefooted, and splash through the carbolic on the floors. This is cholera. These people, lying so quietly upon their hard pillows, have cholera. It is not spectacular. All are poor folk, fishermen, sailors, farmers, shopkeepers, all the ignorant, the stupid, who were not afraid. One is dying. Nose pinched, gasping, bathed in sweat. The hot air can't warm him. He is dying, cold.

So there is cholera in the land, and fear of cholera. Those who were not afraid have cholera. With them it is a matter of a few days only, one way or the other. But those who have fear of cholera have something which lasts much longer, weeks and weeks. Till the heat breaks. Till the typhoon comes.

Ellen Newbold La Motte

COSMIC JUSTICE

Young Withers bought out his uncle's firm of Withers, Ltd., importers. He had been associated with his uncle for some years, as a minor partner, and how he could manage to take over the prosperous Withers, Ltd. without capital, is one of the mysteries of finance that do not concern us. Suffice it that he did, everything included, the big godowns on the quais, shipping rights, the goodwill, stock and fixtures, and the old compradore, Li Yuan Chang. Most particular was old Mr. Withers that Li Yuan Chang should be included. "You will never find a better compradore," he had explained over and over, "in fact, the business will go to pieces without him." Presumably old Mr. Withers knew what he was talking about, for Li had been his interpreter, his accountant, his man of affairs for years. So of course young Withers made no objection, and considered that he was very fortunate in having Li stay with him, after the turnover. For old Li was rich enough to retire by this time, no doubt, as compradores always find means to put away something year by year over and above their salaries. But he was scrupulously honest—old Mr. Withers had full and complete trust in him, and explained to his nephew that he could leave Tientsin from time to time, for as long a time as he liked, in fact, and could be sure meanwhile that old Li would look out for his interests.

"Just be careful of him," he explained. "He's really invaluable. But be a little careful of him—considerate, I mean—he's not very strong—"

"Chandoo?" asked young Withers suspiciously, by which he meant, was Li addicted to smoking that cheapest form of opium, the refuse and scrapings, which was the only grade that all but the richest could afford.

"Oh never," replied old Mr. Withers, "never. In all the years I've had him. Never touches a pipe. Temperate and austere in all things, to a degree. But he is getting old now and needs humouring—likes to feel his importance, does not care to be overlooked in the way young men may be inclined to overlook him,—his work, I mean. Besides, he's not very strong, rather delicate in fact, so you must be easy with him. But you'll never get a better compradore, and he's good for many years yet—or until you learn the ropes."

After which old Mr. Withers concerned himself very earnestly in the preparations for his departure, for he was leaving China for a better land,—England, I mean.

Young Withers set about learning the business under the direction of old Li. Which greatly complimented old Li, who liked being deferred to by a European. And young Withers being very easy-going, and having fallen into a business which required no up-building, being already in its stride, most successful, he left a good many of the details to his compradore, and bragged about him a good deal, saying that indeed he had inherited from his uncle a most wonderful and competent man of affairs. Therefore he was greatly astonished one day, about two years after his accession, when Li asked for a vacation—a long one.

"Want go America," explained the Chinese succinctly. Young Withers was dumbfounded.

"But you can't go America!" he explained, "no can go. What become of business here in Tientsin if you go America? No can do."

Li had had his own way about many things during a great

　　　　Ellen Newbold La Motte

number of years, and opposition, no matter from what motives, meant nothing to him. He settled his big horn spectacles more firmly on his nose, and flecked invisible dust from his rich black brocade coat.

"Want go America," he repeated without emphasis.

"Whatever for?" asked young Withers, to whom a desire to go to America was incomprehensible. He himself had never felt a desire to go to America, and that his old compradore should be so obsessed was past his understanding. Besides, he could imagine somewhat what would befall the old gentleman, who after many years was only able to speak pidgin-English, who never wore European clothes, and who had managed to retain his magnificent queu in spite of all the troubles following the Boxer business. Old Withers had managed to preserve Li's queu for him. Took him into his compound and sheltered him, and finally got a permit from the Legation to allow him to wear it. Li was enormously proud of this queu, which was long and thick and glossy, and its length enhanced by a black silk cord, neatly plaited in towards the end—altogether, it came nearly down to his heels, the envy and admiration of many a Chinese gentleman who had been abruptly shorn before help arrived. Young Withers visualised his dignified compradore the figure of fun to irreverent American crowds. He sincerely wished to preserve him from what he felt must be an unpleasant experience. He was even more anxious to protect his old friend from what would probably be in store for him, than through any selfish desire to retain his services.

"Come back again four month," observed Li. "Not long time. Want to go." Young Withers sighed. It was impossible to explain to the old man. There were pitfalls and pitfalls, he well knew. Yet he had never been to America himself, so could not speak from experience. Only the evening before he had been dining in company with a wise woman of sorts, a French lady who had lived in a cave in Tibet for some years, pursuing reluctant hermits into their mountain fastnesses in order to obtain elucidation on certain Buddhist books. She had told him frankly that she was bound back again for her cave, or for the wilds of Mongolia, but never, under any circumstances, could she trust herself to the risks of American civilization. Young Withers tried to explain something of this to the old man, who was very patient and did not interrupt him, but the seed was falling on barren ground. If he could just understand English better, thought Withers, I might be able to make him see. So Withers' oratory was lost, to a large degree, and when he came to a pause Li repeated, without emphasis,

"Want go America."

"But you're too old!" exclaimed the young man, exasperated by such obstinacy. "Too—you're too—you're not strong enough. You're too—delicate—"

"Want go America. Four month. Come back then," said Li, and Withers gave it up. Two weeks later Li was standing on the deck of a small Japanese liner bound from Tientsin to Kobe, from which port he would transship to a larger Japanese liner bound for San Francisco. He took with him many bundles of odd sizes, wrapped in coarse blue cotton, seemingly of no value. He waved a dignified farewell from the rail, and young Withers, on the dock, watched the departure of his old compradore with infinite misgivings.

Four months, including the passage both ways, proved much too long a time in which to see America. Li returned unexpectedly one day, within half that time, a silent and broken man. His blue bundles, whatever their mystery, were gone, his rich brocade coat was gone, and gone also was his confidence and trust in human kind. Only his thick, glossy, long queue remained to him,—that, and a singular taciturnity. Whatever his experiences, no word would he speak concerning them—he preserved a rigid silence. Something had been broken in the old man, there beyond the seas, and whatever had befallen him was abhorrent and unspeakable. He seemed very much older, very much more frail, and his thin, fine hands were always trembling in a manner unaccustomed.

Young Withers was in distress, for Li's distress was so obvious, his singular reticence making him suffer still more.

"Those thugs in San Francisco must have cleaned out the old fellow first day on shore," he concluded, and then thought no more about it. It was pitiful to see the old man, however, pitiful to watch him going about his duties with the recollection of his terrible days in the New World under-mining his spirits and vitality. The secret, whatever it was that had befallen him, was sapping his frail strength. Only on one occasion, several months later, did he bring up the subject. He appeared suddenly before Withers' desk one day, and there was an angry gleam in his spectacled eyes.

"Your uncle never let me go America. Twenty years with your uncle. Very good man. Never can go." He turned away abruptly.

"By Jove," thought young Withers to himself, "the old chap's holding me responsible. Blaming it all on me. I like that!" and he laughed a little, uneasily. These Chinese were queer ones. You never knew how they stood.

The firm of Withers, Ltd. was very busy. Every week or so ships came into the harbour with boxes and bales of European merchandise of a rather shoddy kind, intended for the markets of North China. And there was much business in transferring these boxes and bales to the big godowns, with their heavy iron doors and windows, in checking them up, sorting them out— in short, all the sort of activity that goes with a firm of importers, such as this one. Also there was much business in distributing these boxes and bales, or rather the contents thereof, to the railway station, for shipment to Peking and to remote provinces in the north and west. In Peking, these shoddy goods were made into smaller bales, and laden on camels, for some far off, remote destination in the interior. This took Withers frequently to Peking, leaving old Li in charge of the godowns in Tientsin. Withers always took charge of this end of the business, because of the opportunity it offered to get away from daily contact with his old compradore. Somehow, he felt rather uneasy in the old man's presence. There was a change in his manner, most marked. Again and again that remark occurred to him, and again and again, in the compradore's presence, Withers was conscious of a feeling of undefinable hostility. He holds me responsible, he thought, absurd, but that's what it is. Because I did not prevent him from going to America. Therefore Withers was very glad to go to Peking from time to time, for he liked the excitement of the barbaric capital, and besides, he thought it would be good for Li to be quite on his own in charge of the godowns, and might distract his thoughts from that obsession which was preying upon him.

One day, after an absence of two weeks, young Withers returned to his Tientsin office, which wore a somewhat deserted air. The shroff was clicking on his abacus, and left off snicking the beads up and down to remark casually that the compradore had gone. The shroff was a young Chinese who spoke excellent, mission-school English, and wore good European clothes, and he shared Withers' astonishment that such a thing had happened.

"Wanted to go home, he said. Had had enough business. Gone home ten days ago, with his family. Said say good-bye to you."

Withers' first feeling was of relief. That's that, he thought to himself, and just as well. He stood eyeing the young Chinese accountant, and the shroff looked him back fairly in the eye, and the same thought passed through both minds. A younger man would do just as well as compradore, and here was the younger man at hand, waiting. "Let's go down to the godowns," said Withers, and the two walked out of the office together, in the direction of the quais. The shroff should learn things from the beginning, and taking charge of the bales and boxes in the warehouses, counting them, distributing their contents, was part of the business.

On unlocking the great, heavy doors, the godowns presented a singular aspect. Never, in all the years that young Withers had been associated as junior partner in Withers, Ltd., and never in the few years since he had become Withers, Ltd. himself, had the godowns presented such an aspect. They were empty. Quite, stark, utterly empty. Not a bale, not a box, not a yard of calico was to be found anywhere about. The sunshine slanted in through the open door, and not a moat of dust danced in the rays, for nothing had been disturbed for some time, and the dust was settled. They went top-side, into the lofts. The same thoroughness presented itself. Everything had been cleared out, absolutely.

"Stolen!" exclaimed Withers.

"Clean-sweep!" said the shroff, in his mission-school English.

"Ruined!" added Withers to himself.

Together they hurried back to the office and examined things. It was evident in a moment how it had been done. Withers had signed an order for the removal of five boxes. The compradore had deftly added a cipher and raised it to fifty. And so on. Done repeatedly, with neatness and precision, over Withers' own signature. No wonder the streets about the godowns had presented an air of activity at times.

"We must find him," said Withers, "catch him quickly, before he has time to dispose of the money."

The old compradore had made no effort to hide his whereabouts. There were a dozen people to whom he had said farewell, telling them that he had now given up work and was retiring with his family to his home in the Western Hills. Over Jehol way. Three weeks by cart. Aye, his cart had come down from Peking to fetch him, a two days' journey. He was not taking the train. He had started early one morning in his big, blue-hooded cart, drawn by a gorgeous yellow mule, its harness inlaid with jade stones. Not number-one jade, of course, but still jade, and of value. Ten days ago he had gone.

Withers and the shroff caught the first train out for Peking, and arriving in two hours, made hasty preparations for their journey. They obtained a cart and a mule, bedding rolls and tinned food, and by afternoon had set out through the West Gate of the Tartar City, over the dusty plains towards the Western Hills. Over Jehol way, towards a village beyond Jehol, up in the hills, where Li Yuan Chang had his dwelling.

Travelling is slow in a Peking cart, and uncomfortable. The heavy, springless vehicle lumbered along, bouncing over the deep, dried ruts, at times sinking hub deep into the dry holes. There were times when the road was below the level of the adjacent fields, so deep below that even the hood of the cart was below them, worn as they were by centuries of travel. At these times, the dust swept through the narrow channel, blinding. Once or twice they ran into a dust storm whirling down from the north, from the great Gobi Desert, beyond. Then they drew down the curtains of the cart, suffocating inside, tossed from side to side, up and down, by the hard jolting of the vehicle. By night they rested at wayside inns, sometimes finding the compounds filled with camels, great shaggy brutes that lay about at all angles, over the courtyard, and snorted and nipped at the intruders. They slept at night in their cart, wrapping up well in their bedding rolls, shivering at times in the keen October wind. Their coolies shared the k'ang within, with the camel drivers and other travellers, but Withers and the shroff preferred the cart, for there were worse if smaller animals than camels to be found in native hostelries. Toilsome, weary days succeeded one another, broken by restless nights, yet ever they pushed westward, slowly, laboriously.

The coolies brought them news of the wayside, gathering it each night from the inns. A great mandarin had passed that way some days ago—a great man surely, to judge by the length of the axles of his cart, which stuck out a good foot beyond the hubs, marking him as a man of importance. And a great yellow mule, with harness set with jade stones, and the brasses polished,—oh, a very rich man, evidently! So each night they heard accounts of the rich man who had gone ahead, with his retinue, his family and servants and packmules. It was well noised abroad, evidently, through the countryside. Travellers coming from beyond Jehol had met him with his train, and the inns at which they stopped always had news of his progress, outward bound. In a hurry, too. And very fearful of the roadside dangers. Always in the compounds before dusk, fearful of highwaymen.

To Withers, the suspense of the slow journey was well nigh unbearable. He, too, was in a hurry, worn with fatigue and anxiety. At first, he had been merely anxious to overtake the old man, to obtain restitution. But with the wayside gossip prevailing, other fears entered his mind. One day at noon time, they entered a village apparently deserted. The heavy gates of the compounds were closed, not a person visible in the long, straggling street. Every one had withdrawn himself into his house, behind locked and bolted doors. At the inn, they pounded repeatedly on the gates, asking admission. Slowly, after a very long time, the gates were opened an inch, and it could be seen that there was the pressure of many men on the inside, ready to slam and bar them in an instant. Then, seeing they were but travellers, they were hastily admitted into the courtyard, and the gates closed and barred again. Bandits. A band of them was scouring the country, thirty or more, down from Mongolia. Abject terror was on every face. The whole village was under its spell.

"We must push on," said Withers, "we must hasten." The shroff was very fearful, but as he was to be compradore now, to do the work of a European, he could not show fear. But the mafu and the coolies were too frightened to continue the journey, so they were left behind, and Withers and the shroff went off by themselves. It was very foolhardy, he told himself, it was sheer madness. But he was ruined anyhow, so it did not much matter. Only, he must somehow reach the village three days' journey beyond Jehol—if only he could arrive in time.

Very laborious was the travelling, and they walked in the wake of fear. They now passed through many deserted villages, one after another, locked and barred, that the murderous band from Mongolia had ridden through. Only, they had gone ahead, the bandits—perhaps they would not be riding back that way again. Perhaps they would be going on, into the north again, after they had finished—

Finished? Yes, it was a very rich man they were after,—they had asked for him all along the road. They were trailing him to his home, following with great ease the description of the great mandarin, with the great yellow mule with jade-set harness, who had gone by with his retinue just before.

So Withers and the shroff continued their desolate journey, day by day, across the plains, over such roads as are not, save in North China. Passing through villages shut and empty, through fields in which there were no workers, following in the train of terror that had been spread over the land by the bandits from the north. And the terror reached into Withers' heart, making it cold. They do not want *us*, he said to himself, over and over. We are quite safe. But the old man— The little shroff, however, who was also filled with terror, did not think they were safe at all. Only he must appear as brave as a European, so he could only tremble inwardly. Besides all that, the big mule was very difficult to manage, and they had to drag the cart from the deep ruts many times a day, and each evening when they were most tired, they had to calm the suspicions of those within, and make long explanations before the inn gates, before they could be admitted into the compounds.

They arrived at their destination at dusk one evening, after three weeks' weary travel. Trembling fingers pointed out the house—trembling, but in a manner, reassured. At the end of the long street they would find the house, a very fine house indeed—formerly a mandarin's palace, they explained, but purchased a few months ago by a rich man who had come there with his family to live. The tired men and tired mule pushed on through the long street, gazed upon curiously by clustering Chinese, huddled in doorways. They came to a high

Ellen Newbold La Motte

wall topped with broken glass, a high, strong wall, surrounding a large compound. Beyond, at the entrance, stood two stone lions, such as mark the homes of the rich and great. But the great stone guardian lions were guarding a broken door. The high, red lacquered door was split into many pieces, the hinges holding, but the doors themselves split, so that a man's body could crawl through.

Withers led the way, the shroff following. Within, the compound was deserted. They made their way to the doors of the main house, which had been smashed in. The rooms inside were empty, stripped, their treasures gone, cleaned out. Very much in appearance like the godowns in Tientsin. They made their way through the silent compound into the women's compound in the rear. It was the same—ransacked, despoiled. But there were many compounds and many houses, so together they passed through moon gates, over elaborate terraces, beside peony mountains, and summer houses, across delicate rock bridges with marble balustrades. Silent, deserted, bearing the evidence of thorough looting.

Then, quite at the rear, a woman appeared, the number-one wife of Li Yuan Chang. She peered round the edges of a moon gate, hiding her body behind it. She recognised Withers and the shroff and came forward. She was very apologetic, very embarrassed, for she was wearing coolie clothes. Her own, she explained, had been taken from her by the bandits. Timidly she approached them, but the timidity was embarrassment. She was very embarrassed to be found in coolie clothes, felt resentment at the humiliation, and apologised repeatedly for her appearance. She could think of nothing else. Then she led the way still further to the rear, to a compound quite behind all the other compounds and other houses of the gorgeous mandarin's palace. The last stand of the defenders. They were scattered about the courtyard in all attitudes, in grotesque and uncouth positions, all dead. She pointed to a figure lying face downward, a thin, elderly figure, in blood-soaked black brocade, with a magnificent queu lying at right angles to the dead body.

Once more she apologised for appearing before the gentlemen in coolie clothes. She felt the disgrace keenly.

"My husband," she explained contemptuously, pointing to the old compradore, "was unable to protect us. He was always such a delicate old thing."

Choose from Thousands of 1stWorldLibrary Classics By

A. M. Barnard	Booth Tarkington	Edward Everett Hale
Ada Leverson	Boyd Cable	Edward J. O'Biren
Adolphus William Ward	Bram Stoker	Edward S. Ellis
Aesop	C. Collodi	Edwin L. Arnold
Agatha Christie	C. E. Orr	Eleanor Atkins
Alexander Aaronsohn	C. M. Ingleby	Eleanor Hallowell Abbott
Alexander Kielland	Carolyn Wells	Eliot Gregory
Alexandre Dumas	Catherine Parr Traill	Elizabeth Gaskell
Alfred Gatty	Charles A. Eastman	Elizabeth McCracken
Alfred Ollivant	Charles Amory Beach	Elizabeth Von Arnim
Alice Duer Miller	Charles Dickens	Ellem Key
Alice Turner Curtis	Charles Dudley Warner	Emerson Hough
Alice Dunbar	Charles Farrar Browne	Emilie F. Carlen
Allen Chapman	Charles Ives	Emily Bronte
Alleyne Ireland	Charles Kingsley	Emily Dickinson
Ambrose Bierce	Charles Klein	Enid Bagnold
Amelia E. Barr	Charles Hanson Towne	Enilor Macartney Lane
Amory H. Bradford	Charles Lathrop Pack	Erasmus W. Jones
Andrew Lang	Charles Romyn Dake	Ernie Howard Pie
Andrew McFarland Davis	Charles Whibley	Ethel May Dell
Andy Adams	Charles Willing Beale	Ethel Turner
Angela Brazil	Charlotte M. Braeme	Ethel Watts Mumford
Anna Alice Chapin	Charlotte M. Yonge	Eugene Sue
Anna Sewell	Charlotte Perkins Stetson	Eugenie Foa
Annie Besant	Clair W. Hayes	Eugene Wood
Annie Hamilton Donnell	Clarence Day Jr.	Eustace Hale Ball
Annie Payson Call	Clarence E. Mulford	Evelyn Everett-green
Annie Roe Carr	Clemence Housman	Everard Cotes
Annonaymous	Confucius	F. H. Cheley
Anton Chekhov	Coningsby Dawson	F. J. Cross
Archibald Lee Fletcher	Cornelis DeWitt Wilcox	F. Marion Crawford
Arnold Bennett	Cyril Burleigh	Fannie E. Newberry
Arthur C. Benson	D. H. Lawrence	Federick Austin Ogg
Arthur Conan Doyle	Daniel Defoe	Ferdinand Ossendowski
Arthur M. Winfield	David Garnett	Fergus Hume
Arthur Ransome	Dinah Craik	Florence A. Kilpatrick
Arthur Schnitzler	Don Carlos Janes	Fremont B. Deering
Arthur Train	Donald Keyhoe	Francis Bacon
Atticus	Dorothy Kilner	Francis Darwin
B.H. Baden-Powell	Dougan Clark	Frances Hodgson Burnett
B. M. Bower	Douglas Fairbanks	Frances Parkinson Keyes
B. C. Chatterjee	E. Nesbit	Frank Gee Patchin
Baroness Emmuska Orczy	E. P. Roe	Frank Harris
Baroness Orczy	E. Phillips Oppenheim	Frank Jewett Mather
Basil King	E. S. Brooks	Frank L. Packard
Bayard Taylor	Earl Barnes	Frank V. Webster
Ben Macomber	Edgar Rice Burroughs	Frederic Stewart Isham
Bertha Muzzy Bower	Edith Van Dyne	Frederick Trevor Hill
Bjornstjerne Bjornson	Edith Wharton	Frederick Winslow Taylor

Friedrich Kerst	Hayden Carruth	James Branch Cabell
Friedrich Nietzsche	Helent Hunt Jackson	James DeMille
Fyodor Dostoyevsky	Helen Nicolay	James Joyce
G.A. Henty	Hendrik Conscience	James Lane Allen
G.K. Chesterton	Hendy David Thoreau	James Lane Allen
Gabrielle E. Jackson	Henri Barbusse	James Oliver Curwood
Garrett P. Serviss	Henrik Ibsen	James Oppenheim
Gaston Leroux	Henry Adams	James Otis
George A. Warren	Henry Ford	James R. Driscoll
George Ade	Henry Frost	Jane Abbott
Geroge Bernard Shaw	Henry James	Jane Austen
George Cary Eggleston	Henry Jones Ford	Jane L. Stewart
George Durston	Henry Seton Merriman	Janet Aldridge
George Ebers	Henry W Longfellow	Jens Peter Jacobsen
George Eliot	Herbert A. Giles	Jerome K. Jerome
George Gissing	Herbert Carter	Jessie Graham Flower
George MacDonald	Herbert N. Casson	John Buchan
George Meredith	Herman Hesse	John Burroughs
George Orwell	Hildegard G. Frey	John Cournos
George Sylvester Viereck	Homer	John F. Kennedy
George Tucker	Honore De Balzac	John Gay
George W. Cable	Horace B. Day	John Glasworthy
George Wharton James	Horace Walpole	John Habberton
Gertrude Atherton	Horatio Alger Jr.	John Joy Bell
Gordon Casserly	Howard Pyle	John Kendrick Bangs
Grace E. King	Howard R. Garis	John Milton
Grace Gallatin	Hugh Lofting	John Philip Sousa
Grace Greenwood	Hugh Walpole	John Taintor Foote
Grant Allen	Humphry Ward	Jonas Lauritz Idemil Lie
Guillermo A. Sherwell	Ian Maclaren	Jonathan Swift
Gulielma Zollinger	Inez Haynes Gillmore	Joseph A. Altsheler
Gustav Flaubert	Irving Bacheller	Joseph Carey
H. A. Cody	Isabel Cecilia Williams	Joseph Conrad
H. B. Irving	Isabel Hornibrook	Joseph E. Badger Jr
H.C. Bailey	Israel Abrahams	Joseph Hergesheimer
H. G. Wells	Ivan Turgenev	Joseph Jacobs
H. H. Munro	J.G.Austin	Jules Vernes
H. Irving Hancock	J. Henri Fabre	Julian Hawthrone
H. R. Naylor	J. M. Barrie	Julie A Lippmann
H. Rider Haggard	J. M. Walsh	Justin Huntly McCarthy
H. W. C. Davis	J. Macdonald Oxley	Kakuzo Okakura
Haldeman Julius	J. R. Miller	Karle Wilson Baker
Hall Caine	J. S. Fletcher	Kate Chopin
Hamilton Wright Mabie	J. S. Knowles	Kenneth Grahame
Hans Christian Andersen	J. Storer Clouston	Kenneth McGaffey
Harold Avery	J. W. Duffield	Kate Langley Bosher
Harold McGrath	Jack London	Kate Langley Bosher
Harriet Beecher Stowe	Jacob Abbott	Katherine Cecil Thurston
Harry Castlemon	James Allen	Katherine Stokes
Harry Coghill	James Andrews	L. A. Abbot
Harry Houidini	James Baldwin	L. T. Meade

L. Frank Baum
Latta Griswold
Laura Dent Crane
Laura Lee Hope
Laurence Housman
Lawrence Beasley
Leo Tolstoy
Leonid Andreyev
Lewis Carroll
Lewis Sperry Chafer
Lilian Bell
Lloyd Osbourne
Louis Hughes
Louis Joseph Vance
Louis Tracy
Louisa May Alcott
Lucy Fitch Perkins
Lucy Maud Montgomery
Luther Benson
Lydia Miller Middleton
Lyndon Orr
M. Corvus
M. H. Adams
Margaret E. Sangster
Margret Howth
Margaret Vandercook
Margaret W. Hungerford
Margret Penrose
Maria Edgeworth
Maria Thompson Daviess
Mariano Azuela
Marion Polk Angellotti
Mark Overton
Mark Twain
Mary Austin
Mary Catherine Crowley
Mary Cole
Mary Hastings Bradley
Mary Roberts Rinehart
Mary Rowlandson
M. Wollstonecraft Shelley
Maud Lindsay
Max Beerbohm
Myra Kelly
Nathaniel Hawthrone
Nicolo Machiavelli
O. F. Walton
Oscar Wilde

Owen Johnson
P.G. Wodehouse
Paul and Mabel Thorne
Paul G. Tomlinson
Paul Severing
Percy Brebner
Percy Keese Fitzhugh
Peter B. Kyne
Plato
Quincy Allen
R. Derby Holmes
R. L. Stevenson
R. S. Ball
Rabindranath Tagore
Rahul Alvares
Ralph Bonehill
Ralph Henry Barbour
Ralph Victor
Ralph Waldo Emmerson
Rene Descartes
Ray Cummings
Rex Beach
Rex E. Beach
Richard Harding Davis
Richard Jefferies
Richard Le Gallienne
Robert Barr
Robert Frost
Robert Gordon Anderson
Robert L. Drake
Robert Lansing
Robert Lynd
Robert Michael Ballantyne
Robert W. Chambers
Rosa Nouchette Carey
Rudyard Kipling
Saint Augustine
Samuel B. Allison
Samuel Hopkins Adams
Sarah Bernhardt
Sarah C. Hallowell
Selma Lagerlof
Sherwood Anderson
Sigmund Freud
Standish O'Grady
Stanley Weyman
Stella Benson
Stella M. Francis

Stephen Crane
Stewart Edward White
Stijn Streuvels
Swami Abhedananda
Swami Parmananda
T. S. Ackland
T. S. Arthur
The Princess Der Ling
Thomas A. Janvier
Thomas A Kempis
Thomas Anderton
Thomas Bailey Aldrich
Thomas Bulfinch
Thomas De Quincey
Thomas Dixon
Thomas H. Huxley
Thomas Hardy
Thomas More
Thornton W. Burgess
U. S. Grant
Upton Sinclair
Valentine Williams
Various Authors
Vaughan Kester
Victor Appleton
Victor G. Durham
Victoria Cross
Virginia Woolf
Wadsworth Camp
Walter Camp
Walter Scott
Washington Irving
Wilbur Lawton
Wilkie Collins
Willa Cather
Willard F. Baker
William Dean Howells
William le Queux
W. Makepeace Thackeray
William W. Walter
William Shakespeare
Winston Churchill
Yei Theodora Ozaki
Yogi Ramacharaka
Young E. Allison
Zane Grey

www.ingramcontent.com/pod-product-compliance
Lightning Source LLC
Chambersburg PA
CBHW051842170626
46807CB00003B/1313